"Do you want to try out the sex survey?" Brooke asked

Marc glanced at the magazine, then at Brooke. His eyes grew dark. "I'm game if you are. But no cheating."

Brooke wrinkled her nose at him. "I don't cheat."

"That's good to hear." He stretched out on his side, propped his head in his palm and patted the sleeping bag in front of him. "Still, I think you'd better come down here so I can look into your eyes when you answer," he said, grinning.

She hesitated for a moment, then scooted down until she lay on her side facing him. They weren't touching physically, but a keen sense of intimacy surrounded them.

"Okay," he said. "Let's get started." He paused over the questions, deliberating which one to choose. "Here's a good one," he said. " 'If someone completely turned you on, would you consider having a hot fling with them?' "

Brooke's skin tingled. The question addressed an issue they'd been avoiding since yesterday morning's kiss. With her new motto, Just Do It, ringing in her head, she answered, "Well...yes, I guess I've considered it." She gathered up her courage and looked him in the eye. *"With you."*

Dear Reader,

The title, *Tempted,* just about sums up the premise of this book. When my sensible heroine, Brooke Jamison, finds herself stranded with her very sexy ex-brother-in-law, Marc, she can't resist the temptation to shed her inhibitions and indulge in a few of her favorite erotic fantasies. Two days of blissful confinement changes everything between them, but can she risk her heart on a man who is as commitment-shy as they come?

Hot, sexy, erotic... Those are the elements inherent in the BLAZE subseries that allowed me to push personal boundaries and make this one of my most sizzling books to date. I hope you enjoy Brooke and Marc's story, their sensual journey and the passionate discoveries they make along the way.

And be sure to watch for my next ultra-sexy Temptation BLAZE novel, *Seduced,* available in December 2000. Meanwhile, I'd love to know what you think of *Tempted.* You can write to me at P.O. Box 1102, Rialto, CA 92377-1102. I always write back! For a list of upcoming releases, check out my Web site at www.janelledenison.com.

Fondly,

Janelle Denison

Books by Janelle Denison

HARLEQUIN TEMPTATION

TEMPTED
Janelle Denison

HARLEQUIN®

TORONTO • NEW YORK • LONDON
AMSTERDAM • PARIS • SYDNEY • HAMBURG
STOCKHOLM • ATHENS • TOKYO • MILAN • MADRID
PRAGUE • WARSAW • BUDAPEST • AUCKLAND

To Carly Phillips and Julie Elizabeth Leto,
for your extraordinary friendship
and unending encouragement.
Viva las Divas!

And to Don, for understanding that our
astronomical long distance phone bill
is a legitimate business expense.

ISBN 0-373-25899-2

TEMPTED

Copyright © 2000 by Janelle Denison.

Prologue

"THIRTY-FIVE YEARS of marriage. Are you as impressed as I am?"

The deep, masculine baritone murmuring into her ear from over her shoulder caused Brooke Jamison to shiver. She turned and faced the owner of that sexy voice—her former brother-in-law, Marc Jamison. She met warm gray eyes framed in sooty lashes, and a mouth tipped in a lazy, sexy smile that was as natural as his gregarious personality. His thick, black hair, looking as soft and enticing as midnight, had been tousled by the slight breeze cooling the early August evening. In an attempt to maintain an executive image for his electrical contracting company, he wore his hair short, but the ends that curled over the collar of his sports jacket bespoke the rebel he was.

Startled by the unexpected flutter of awareness that tickled her belly, Brooke focused on his question and her answer. "Your parents' marriage is amazing, and inspiring."

Sliding his hands into the front pockets of his chocolate-colored trousers, Marc looked briefly to the guests gathered in his parents' lavishly decorated backyard to celebrate Kathleen and Doug's thirty-fifth anniversary. "So, are you having a good time?"

"Yeah, I am," she admitted, glad that she'd accepted his mother's invitation to join the celebration. She'd been hesitant at first, considering her and Eric's divorce had been finalized two weeks before, but Kathleen and the rest of the Jamison family had made her feel welcome, including her ex-husband. Despite the inevitable end to their marriage, she and Eric still maintained an amicable relationship, rare among divorced couples. Still, Kathleen's invitation had initially taken her off guard.

"I have to confess I'm surprised your family wanted me here, considering I'm technically not part of the family anymore."

A small frown pulled at his dark brows, her admission obviously causing him concern. "Hey, once you're a Jamison, you're part of the family forever, didn't you know that?"

Brooke smiled, liking the way that sounded. Unfortunately, in her experience families divided when couples split up. The dissension and emotional upheaval her own father had caused when he'd ended his marriage to her mother had been monumental. Without compunction, he'd shattered fragile family ties, forcing Brooke to mature beyond her thirteen years and leaving his other daughter hurt and disillusioned.

"That's not usually the way a divorce works," she returned, taking a sip of her drink.

"You divorced Eric, not the rest of us," he countered easily. "My parents adore you, my mother thinks of you as the daughter she never had, and I think you're pretty special, too."

His complimentary words were simple and sincere, yet she was suddenly, inexplicably entranced by the warm glow in his gaze. Ignoring the odd racing of her pulse, she looked away and found her ex-husband trapped in a steady stream of one-sided dialogue with his uncle George, a boisterous man who reveled in dominating the conversation. The beefy hand resting on Eric's shoulder guaranteed he wasn't going anywhere anytime soon.

Eric's hazel eyes met hers over Uncle George's balding head and silently pleaded, "Have mercy on me, please." He flashed her one of the endearing smiles that had won her over when she'd first met him, but now failed to elicit any stirring of desire or the inclination to help him out of his predicament.

Marc followed her line of vision to his brother and groaned. "Eric looks miserable, and we both know how long-winded, and boring, my uncle can be. Think we ought to go save him?"

An amused smile tipped the corner of her mouth as she considered Marc's question for all of two seconds before breaking eye contact with Eric and leaving him in his uncle's clutches. "No, I don't believe I will," she said without a hint of remorse. "It's no longer my job to rescue Eric, or play the doting wife." He was on his own, as she was. And she was pleased to discover she was fine with that.

Marc studied her expression intently. "You're doing okay, then?"

"More than okay," she verified, nodding. "Though after a two-year marriage, it seems strange to be single and available again."

"I'm sure that status won't last long." He leaned toward her, so close she caught the faint scent of mint on his breath. "Between you and me, Eric never knew a good thing when he saw one. I was really hoping you'd be 'The One.'"

She blinked up at him, not quite understanding what he meant. "'The One'?"

"Yeah, the one woman who could make Eric settle down."

Now it was her turn to frown. There was something in the depth of Marc's eyes she couldn't quite decipher. A hint of disappointment, she realized, but didn't understand its source.

"I'm only one woman," she said. "And that obviously wasn't enough for Eric."

Eric had tried to conform to their wedding vows, but ultimately he'd realized and admitted that he was a man who couldn't commit to any one woman. A genetic flaw, he'd told her, passed on from father to sons. Except Eric's father, Doug, had chosen to make his marriage work after his one indiscretion. Judging by the closeness Doug and Kathleen now seemed to share, their relationship had endured.

Resignation flickered across Marc's lean features. "If that's the case, it doesn't leave much hope for me."

His words held a longing she found curious. In the years that she'd known Marc she'd discovered that he steadfastly avoided serious relationships, didn't commit himself to any one woman and preferred to play the field. He *embraced* bachelorhood.

So why, then, did she get the impression that he wished differently?

Placing her empty glass on the corner of the rented bar, she decided that talk of anniversaries and marriage was getting the best of her and making her come to absurd conclusions about her brother-in-law. Making her feel things she had no business feeling.

She called up a smile. "It's getting late. I'd better say my goodbyes and be on my way."

He nodded, his charming grin lightening the moment. "I'll walk you to the door."

Half an hour later, after an endless round of hugs and farewells from the entire Jamison clan, Marc escorted her to the foyer. He rested his hand lightly at the base of Brooke's spine, the heat of his fingers penetrating through the black linen pants she wore. Her heart thundered in her chest, and she couldn't help but wonder how a simple touch from Marc could evoke such a startling response.

She stepped away from him as inconspicuously as possible when they reached the carved front doors, effectively dislodging that overwhelming contact that had her body tingling. Granted, she'd been without a man for a year, and Marc was extremely attractive, but she'd *never* thought of him as anything more than her husband's brother.

Until now...

His gaze found hers, and the muted sounds of the party faded into the background, making Brooke aware that they were very much alone.

A smile eased across his lips, but his expression was more serious than she'd ever seen it before. "Don't be a stranger, okay?"

Tamping a sudden rush of emotion, she whispered, "Okay."

He gathered her into a warm hug she hadn't even known she needed until she was enveloped by his hard body. Closing her eyes, she breathed deeply, inhaling the scent of warm spice and male heat. Greedily, she leaned into him and absorbed his comforting embrace, reluctant to let the moment go.

As much as she was over Eric, the past year had been difficult, and at times, lonely. She'd moved into her sister's apartment after her separation, and though Jessica provided female companionship, it wasn't enough. With Marc's arms around her, his hands stroking her back, Brooke realized how much she missed something as simple as a man's embrace, a man's touch. Eric had never been very demonstrative in their marriage, believing it wasn't masculine to exhibit tender feelings. Marc had always been one to openly express his affection.

Too soon he pulled back, and she lifted up on her feet to place a chaste kiss on his cheek—the same time he turned his head. Their lips met, momentarily startling them both. Over the past four years she'd shared many platonic kisses with her flirtatious brother-in-law, and this one started as innocently as any, his mouth brushing hers lightly...except somewhere along the way the tenor of the kiss changed, for both of them.

This time his lips lingered a little longer, and his mouth gradually, instinctively, exerted a gentle pressure that surpassed those chaste kisses they'd shared in the past. To her shock, a soft, unexpected moan of pleasure tickled her throat, and his tongue stroked along her bottom lip in tentative exploration.

Her mind spun, her senses reeled, and she struggled to keep her perspective on the situation. Desires and denials clashed, confusing her. Nerve endings that had lain dormant for too long sizzled and came alive. And then she did something incredibly shameless—she touched her tongue to his.

She heard him groan deep in his chest, felt Marc's large hands on her hips guide her backward...until her spine pressed against the wall, and the two of them were shrouded in a shadowy corner. The heat surrounding her was incendiary. She caught a quick glimpse of the sensual hunger glimmering in his eyes and shivered at the thought of being the recipient of all that wild, frenzied electricity.

She didn't protest when he framed her face in his large, callused hands, didn't object or struggle when he lowered his mouth to hers once again. Without preamble, he parted her lips with his, glided his tongue into forbidden territory, and seduced her with one of the hottest, most shockingly intimate kisses she'd ever tasted.

And she let him.

His fingers threaded through her hair, and his thumbs caressed her jaw. Her body swelled, and for a brief moment she felt reckless and wild. The feeling was liberating, exciting...until her conscience rudely reminded her who she was kissing—her bad boy, live-for-the-moment ex-brother-in-law.

Panic edged out pleasure, and she jerked her head back, effectively ending the rapacious kiss, but there was nothing she could do about the slow throb pulsing through her body, making her ache for primitive, erotic things she'd never, *ever* contemplated with Eric. Unfortunately, her ex-husband had never inspired such consuming lust, such excruciating need.

And that knowledge frightened her most of all.

Frantically, she pushed Marc away, and he immediately stepped back. They were both breathing raggedly, and judging by his bewildered expression, he was just as stunned as she was by the instantaneous flare of desire that had leapt between them. *And intrigued*—she recognized the thrill of a challenge in his quicksilver eyes.

Knowing that the dangerous, frivolous kind of interest she saw there could only cause trouble to her heart and emotions, she moved around him in a frenzied blur of motion and fled from the house. She sucked cool night air into her lungs, berating herself for a fool.

"Brooke, wait," she heard his voice, then his clipped steps as he followed her down the brick walkway.

Shaken by what she'd allowed to happen, and refusing to engage in a conversation about her brazen response, she nearly ran to her car. Disengaging her alarm, she slid behind the wheel of her Toyota Four Runner, wincing as his low, exasperated curses reached her. Slamming the door shut, she started the engine, drowning out his voice, then left him standing at the curb with his hands jammed on his hips and his features creased with frustration.

She experienced a twinge of guilt for her abrupt departure, but knew her actions spoke louder than any words possibly could. No matter how much she might want Marc, she wasn't interested in falling for another Jamison.

1

Three months later

"HERE'S TO YOUR NEW single status, Brooke." Stacey Sumner lifted her strawberry margarita in a toast to mark the beginning of their weeklong "girls' retreat" in the Colorado Rocky Mountains.

Brooke grinned at her best friend and co-worker. Clinking her glass with Stacey's and then her sister's, she took a drink of the frothy beverage. "How about a toast to seven days of skiing, soaking in the hot tub, girl talk and eating everything we shouldn't?" At the grocery store on the way up to the time-share cabin she still maintained with Eric, they'd bought enough to satisfy every craving they might have—junk food had definitely been on their agenda.

"Oh, yeah," Jessica agreed, her pale blue eyes sparkling mischievously. "Sounds like heaven."

Stacey reclined on the matching love seat cornering the sofa and crossed her long legs. "Seven days of doing what we want, when we want. Spontaneity is the word for the week."

"And relaxation," Brooke interjected, thinking of all the novels she'd been wanting to read for the past six months and had brought along to curl up with at night.

"Aw, Brooke, you're no fun," Stacey lightly chastised. "This week was supposed to be about spontaneity and shedding inhibitions in celebration of being single again, remember?"

Averting her gaze to the fire crackling in the hearth, Brooke took another drink of her potent margarita. Yeah, she remembered the lecture Stacey had imparted on the drive up to Quail Valley for their ski vacation. But Brooke had always been the quintessential good girl—responsible, dependable and virtuous—thinking long and hard about consequences before acting. She'd even accepted her job as an accountant for Blythe Paints because the position was staid and reliable.

Being reckless wasn't in her psyche...unless she counted that very spontaneous, uninhibited kiss with Marc three months before. Try as she might to forget about that impetuous embrace, the incident, and the man, invaded her thoughts on a daily basis. And at night, well, she'd never had such erotic dreams, had never woken up so on edge. It might have been her own ministrations that had brought her the release her body sought, but it had been Marc who'd starred in the forbidden fantasies she'd woven.

Dismissing the kiss should have been relatively easy, considering she hadn't heard from Marc since that night. It was the way of the Jamison men, to seize the moment, then move on before the situation got too complicated. In this case, it was probably for the best.

Ignoring the heat flushing her skin—from the combined effects of tequila, the warmth of the fire and her sensual memories of Marc—she met Stacey's gaze. "You're the impulsive one, not me," she retorted.

Stacey made a sound of mock disgust. "You're just too exciting for words, Brooke."

She shrugged unapologetically, casually studying her nails. The pale pink polish was chipped and in need of a fresh coat—she planned on treating herself to a manicure and pedicure sometime this week. That's about how exciting her life got. Predictable...and *boring*, she realized.

"Let's try something different, in the way of girl talk," Stacey suggested. "If you could create the perfect, ideal male to be stranded up here with, what qualities would he have and what would he look like? Use your imagination. Fantasize a little."

Unbidden, Brooke's imagination conjured up thick black hair rumpled deliciously, a hard male body made for sin and pleasure, and eyes that darkened from silver to charcoal with a kiss. The fantasies that crowded her mind were something she refused to share with anyone.

Curling her legs beneath her on the sofa cushion, she shoved Marc from her mind and decided to give her ideal male her best shot. "Looks don't really matter," she said honestly, "as long as he's intelligent, warm and humorous."

Stacey braced her elbow on the armrest of the love seat and propped her chin in her hand, giving Brooke and her description of her exemplary mate her undivided attention. "And sexy?"

"In an understated way. Nothing presumptuous or arrogant." She finished off her margarita and thought about one of the things that her own marriage had lacked, and that she had often wished for. "His sole focus would be on me and my needs."

"Oh, yeah," Stacey said in a throaty purr.

Brooke caught her friend's drift right away. "And I don't mean just sexually."

Stacey wriggled her brows suggestively. "Though being focused on sexual needs doesn't hurt."

"I'm talking about emotional needs." She sounded practical and dull, but didn't care. After witnessing what her mother had gone through with her father, and her own experience with Eric, those qualities were important to her. "He'd be a good listener, and not afraid to show his feelings. He'd be secure in his masculinity so he didn't need other women to stroke his ego. And that goes hand in hand with him being monogamous. That's an absolute must."

Which certainly left love-'em-and-leave-'em Marc out of the competition.

"That's very sweet," Jessica said, a bit of awe in her voice. "Do you think men like that actually exist?"

Brooke glanced at her sister, regretting that Jessica's illusions about men had been shattered at such an early age by their father's actions. "Yeah, I do," she said softly, knowing at the same time that it was only her fantasy.

"You're so serious about men." Stacey drained the last of her drink and set her glass on the coffee table in front of her. "Ever thought of just going out and having a wild, mindless affair? Finding some guy that turns you on and having your way with him?"

Brooke imagined ripping Marc's shirt off, buttons flying. She imagined dragging those tight jeans he wore down his hips, pushing him onto his back and straddling his thighs, then seducing him...

Swallowing a groan, she tried to force those erotic images right out of her head, but she couldn't ignore that she *had* wondered a time or two what it would be like to be as sexually liberated as Stacey. To enjoy a man's attentions without pouring a lot of emotion into the relationship. To just lose herself in mutual pleasure with no expectations, no strings, and without the risk of investing that deep, significant part of herself she could never recover once it was offered.

Men did it all the time. Her ex-husband had been guilty of playing that game, but then again, Eric hadn't invested the same emotions that she had into their relationship. She'd learned, belatedly, that he'd been incapable of doing so. She'd discovered, belatedly, that she'd been little more than a challenge for her husband, one he'd conquered, claimed, and quickly grown bored with. She'd determined, belatedly, that commitment wasn't an attribute the men in the Jamison family took seriously.

She *knew* that, so why was she allowing a bad boy like Marc to get under her skin and consume her thoughts?

"I don't think Brooke is that kind of girl," Jessica said when Brooke didn't answer Stacey's question.

The corner of Stacey's mouth tipped up in a lazy, confident smile. "*Everyone* has a wild side. It's just a matter of whether or not they tap into it."

"Very enlightening," Jessica said with a giggle. "And on that note, I think I'll go blend the next batch of margaritas."

Once she'd disappeared into the kitchen, Stacey glanced at Brooke, purpose glimmering in the depths of her eyes. "Ever looked at a guy and thought, I wonder if he's any good in bed?"

Brooke kept her thoughts centered and focused. "No."

Stacey considered that for a moment. "Ever looked at a guy's hands and wondered what they'd feel like sliding over your body?"

Marc had nice hands, large, callused, hot. Her body thrummed at the thought of those palms stroking over her flesh, touching her in sensitive places. "Never."

"Ever looked at a guy's lips and imagined the slow, deep kisses he could give...or maybe the different ways he might use his mouth?"

"No, never." *Liar, liar, liar,* a voice inside Brooke's head chanted.

"Ever heard the phrase, 'just do it'?"

Brooke shrugged. "Yeah."

"It was meant for people like you."

Brooke frowned. "People like me?"

"Yeah, people who are too serious and self-controlled. You need to loosen up so you can get in touch with your feminine needs. 'Just do it' needs to be your new motto—at least for this next week. Then when we return to civilization you can resume looking for that fantasy man of yours."

"Just do it, huh?" Brooke repeated, testing out the words, not sure she could be so unreserved and direct—not when she'd spent her life being responsible and sensible in her approach.

Stacey grinned, looking pleased with herself. "Yeah, whenever you're unsure of something, but you want it really bad, repeat those words. *Just do it.*"

"Just do what?" Jessica asked, returning with a fresh pitcher of strawberry margaritas.

"Anything that strikes your sister's fancy this

week," Stacey said, holding up her glass as Jessica refilled it with the slushy liquid. "Especially when it comes to men."

"Brooke is going man-hunting?" Jessica asked, intrigue infusing her voice.

Brooke winced. "That sounds so...*reckless.*"

"*Impetuous* is a better word, I think." Stacey took a sip of her drink, her eyes bright with sensual knowledge. "You just kind of have to go with the feeling and not analyze the situation from every angle like you do those columns of numbers you work with. If it feels right, just do it."

Brooke chewed on her bottom lip and pondered her friend's suggestion. When it came to men, she'd always been cautious and selective, even analytical. Even her marriage to Eric had been based on practicality rather than uncontrollable passion—on both their parts, she now knew. They'd both had different expectations of their relationship, and each other, and in the end those individual needs had driven them apart emotionally and physically.

Ultimately, she wanted passionate love, a marriage based on mutual respect, and the kind of solid family unit she'd grown up without. She wasn't like Stacey, who dated a slew of men, enjoyed the moment while it lasted, and didn't think about the future. Brooke wanted a future with a man.

One week. Which wasn't a whole lot when she thought of it in terms of the rest of her life stretching ahead of her.

Brooke took a gulp of her margarita, her mind spinning. Could she shed her inhibitions and have a hot,

wild, unemotional fling with a stranger before returning to her stable life and dependable job?

"Tell you what," Stacey said easily, as if sensing her
doubts, "starting tomorrow, we'll check out the prospects on the slopes and see what's out there. If sparks
happen, then go for it. If they don't, no loss."

Sparks, like the kind Marc generated. She shivered at
the thought.

"Since I don't ski, you two are on your own," Jessica
said, settling back on the couch. "I'm going to enjoy the
peace and quiet in the cabin and get caught up on my
medical transcripts."

"Then it's you and me, Brooke." Stacey grinned, lifting her glass in another toast. "And a mountain full of
men to choose from."

Brooke groaned as three glasses clinked together,
trying to keep an open mind about Stacey's man-
hunting plan and her new motto for the week.

Just do it.

"JUST DO IT," Brooke murmured to herself, trying to in-
ject some enthusiasm into her voice as she wiped the
coffee table of the remnants of their afternoon marga-
rita-fest while Stacey and Jessica cleaned the kitchen.
The words sounded flat and dull, too much like her
personal life.

She snorted in disgust. For the past year she'd buried
herself in her work, grasping on to the monotony of her
job to counterbalance the stress and disappointment of
her divorce. And now here she was, starting a new
phase in her life...and still clinging to the safe and familiar.

Dull. Boring. Too damned predictable.

She sighed and straightened the sofa cushions. What Stacey was suggesting went against her grain and all those good-girl qualities she'd lived with her entire life, but much to her own surprise, she was gradually warming to the idea of finding a guy who turned her on and indulging in a sexy interlude. And she hoped in the process she'd finally banish Marc from her mind and ease the sexual frustration he'd caused her for the past three months.

Yeah, that particular idea definitely had merit. And maybe she'd return to Denver with a new attitude and a new outlook on her future.

A beam of headlights slashed through the windows facing the front of the small cabin, cutting through the shadows of twilight. She heard the crunch of snow beneath tires, an engine rumbling as it idled, then everything went quiet.

Curious, she headed toward the window next to the front door and pushed aside the curtain to peer outside. Even bathed in early November dusk, she immediately recognized the vehicle parked next to her Four Runner, a black Suburban with the Jamison Electrical logo emblazoned on the door in bold, white print.

Her heart dropped to her stomach as the object of her lustful fantasies slid from the driver's side of the vehicle. Another male figure emerged from the passenger side, and finally, a third stepped from the back door, his boots crunching on the snow. Marc said something to the two other men, and while the duo moved toward the back of the utility vehicle, Marc started for the cabin's front porch.

Brooke's pulse tripped all over itself. Abruptly, she dropped the curtain and groaned, unable to believe her private refuge was about to be invaded by roughly six hundred pounds of gorgeous male testosterone, two hundred of which was trouble with a capital *T*.

Of all the possible ironies!

Knowing it was inevitable she face him, she opened the door before he had a chance to insert his key into the lock. His hand stopped midair, and their gazes met. A slow, intimate smile claimed his mouth, and his gaze drifted down the length of her with a slow, natural ease that came from years of assessing a woman in a single glance.

Not only did he assess her, he seemed to brand her with a breathless heat wherever his gaze roamed—and it covered plenty of territory in an amazingly short span of time. She found his bold perusal unnerving; the fluttering deep in her belly was equally disconcerting. There was something different in the way he looked at her now, something that was distinctly male, a trifle dangerous and a whole lot predatory.

Her skin tightened, and to her dismay her breasts responded to his visual caress. They swelled within the lacy cups of her bra in a purely feminine way, pushing her taut nipples against the soft cotton of her University of Colorado sweatshirt. Even her thighs and legs seemed to become sensitized to the soft, faded denim of her jeans.

She blamed her body's response on the cold, brisk air filtering into the cabin, but had no such excuse for the contrasting heat warming her in more intimate places—a feverlike flush generated by a pair of smoky-gray eyes. That gaze radiated a sexy, unmistakable kind of message that told her the kiss they'd shared three months ago was a prelude to a deeper kind of magic.

"Hello, Brooke," he greeted her warmly. His voice was deep, rich, and sent a delicious shiver shimmering through her. Good grief, one kiss and now his voice had the ability to seduce her senses and make her weak in the knees.

She struggled to shake the awareness that had her in its grip. "What are you doing here?" she asked, part demand, part curiosity.

Marc lifted black brows over amused eyes. "I should be asking you the same thing. We're here because we borrowed the cabin from Eric until next Tuesday to go skiing. Business is slow right now, so we thought we'd take advantage of the prime skiing conditions."

One glance at the top of his Suburban revealed three pairs of skis strapped to a rack. "Oh, no you don't," she said, shaking her finger at him. "The cabin is *ours* for the week."

He tipped his head and a dark, unruly lock of hair slipped over his forehead. "Did you tell Eric you were coming up?"

A sigh unraveled out of her, fringed with frustration. "Of course I did."

"That's odd." He absently rubbed his thumb along his jaw. "I asked him just this morning if the cabin was free, and he said since he hadn't heard from you, that it must be."

Unease slithered through Brooke, settling in her stomach like a rock. "I left a specific message with his secretary three days ago that I was taking the cabin for the week."

Marc's broad shoulders lifted in an apologetic shrug.

"He obviously didn't get it, Brooke. His secretary is new and, well, she's more beauty than brains, if you get my drift. You know Eric wouldn't deliberately sabotage your plans if he knew you'd be here."

Brooke knew Marc spoke the truth. For all her ex-husband's faults, he wasn't one to do something so underhanded.

Marc's two friends climbed the porch stairs, duffel bags in hand and congenial smiles in place. They flanked Marc and waited for her to invite them into the warmth of the cabin.

She stood guard at the door, certain once the trio invaded the cozy, two-bedroom time-share her chance at a relaxing vacation would vanish. "You can't stay here."

"We don't really have a choice," Marc replied easily. "I called all the resorts in the area, and because of the recent snowfall, everything is completely booked up this weekend. That's why I asked Eric if I could borrow the cabin."

His argument was solid, and believable. Still, Brooke didn't budge.

"Who's here, Brooke?"

The sound of Jessica's curious voice loosened some of the tension building within Brooke. She glanced over her shoulder, watching as her sister exited the kitchen, followed by Stacey.

"*Men,*" Brooke said, the word escaping like the curse it was.

Marc's deep, familiar chuckle strummed down her spine like caressing fingers. Shaking off her reaction, Brooke turned back to the trio, her gaze locking on Marc's. "I don't know what you find so amusing, Jamison, considering you and your friends might be camping in your Suburban for the weekend."

That earned her a sexy grin that made her stomach dip and her toes curl. "You wouldn't do that to me."

He sounded too sure of himself. And her.

Before she could issue a retort, Stacey moved to her side, too much enthusiasm glimmering in her eyes. "Aw, come on, Brooke. These guys have obviously been on the road for a few hours, the least we can do is let them rest before sending them on their way." Her friend extended her hand and introduced herself, beating out any argument Brooke could have issued. "By the way, I'm Stacey Sumner. I work with Brooke at Blythe Paints."

Marc slipped his hand into Stacey's. "Marc Jamison," he said, nodding in acknowledgment.

Stacey flashed a grin. "Ahh, the ex."

"Excuse me?"

"Ex-brother-in-law," Stacey clarified.

A smile quirked his too-sensual mouth as his gaze slid back to Brooke. "I'd like to think I'm still a friend."

Friends don't kiss friends the way you kissed me. Squashing the frisson of heat spiraling toward her belly, despite the chill filling the room from outside, Brooke gave him a tight smile in return. "You're currently a pain in the ass," she muttered.

One of the men standing beside Marc grinned in amusement, and the other coughed to cover up a laugh.

Marc blinked, not the least bit offended. "But a darn loveable one."

"That's debatable," she countered swiftly, refusing to let his compelling charm soften her.

"That's exactly what Brooke needs these days. A good debate." Stacey grabbed Marc's arm and tugged him across the threshold. "Come on in, so we can continue this conversation without the threat of frostbite."

Before Brooke could protest, the cabin was filled with three overwhelmingly masculine bodies, and the small living room seemed to shrink in size.

Marc shrugged out of his jacket and went about introducing his friends, mostly for Stacey's and Jessica's benefit. "This is Shane Hendricks, who works for my company as an electrical engineer," he said of the blond-haired guy who'd seemingly captured Stacey's attention, then nodded toward the other dark-haired man. "And this is Ryan Matthews, a divorce attorney for Haywood and Irwin."

"Nice to meet you all," Stacey said gregariously.

Jessica greeted Shane politely, then turned to Ryan. "An attorney, huh?" A sly smile curved her mouth as Ryan confirmed her question with a nod. "What's black and brown and looks good on a lawyer?" Before he could respond to her odd, unexpected question, she offered the punch line. "A Doberman pinscher."

Brooke groaned, Marc chuckled, and Ryan stared at Jessica in bafflement, taken aback.

Then he shook his head and laughed, too. "Nice greeting. I have to admit I haven't heard that one before."

"Oh, I have one for just about every occasion." With a jaunty spring to her step, Jessica went to the coffee table, picked up her laptop computer and glanced at Brooke. "I'll be up in the loft working on my transcripts until you get everything settled with Marc and his friends."

Interest gleamed in Ryan's gaze as he watched Jessica climb the stairs to the cabin's only second-story bedroom. Once she was out of his line of vision, he looked back at Brooke, a grin quirking his mouth. "Was it something I said?"

Brooke rubbed the slow throb beginning in her temple, and offered the man a reassuring smile. "It's not you, personally. Lawyer jokes are Jessica's specialty. She finds them...amusing." But Brooke knew where Jessica's comments came from. Ryan's profession made him an easy target for the pent-up emotions Jessica had kept deeply buried since their childhood.

As for her own emotions, they were currently under siege, as well. She thought about her forbidden attraction to Marc, her sister's arsenal of lawyer jokes, and Stacey's preoccupation with Shane as he helped her rekindle the fire in the hearth. Combining all that volatile sexual energy and masculine appeal and cramming it into one tiny cabin was not conducive to the rest and leisure she'd envisioned. No, it was more suited to insanity.

Desperate to see the trio on their way, she turned back to the leader of the pack. "Can I talk to you, Marc, alone?" Before he could refuse her, she headed purposefully toward the kitchen, the only room that would provide them a modicum of privacy.

She was determined that, within the next hour, Marc and his friends would be gone and her relaxing, week-long ski retreat would resume as planned.

2

MARC RELEASED a low, deep breath and watched Brooke head toward the kitchen. His gaze was unerringly drawn to the subtle sway of her slim hips, and the way her soft, faded jeans contoured to her curved bottom...which, admittedly, was his favorite part of the female anatomy—long, slender legs taking a close second. But her deeper, less superficial qualities were what tied him up in knots and had his conscience warning him to put her, and the spontaneous kiss they'd shared, out of his mind.

Intensely loyal and infinitely giving, Brooke was exactly the kind of woman he steadfastly avoided. She was so completely opposite from the enjoy-the-moment-while-it-lasts kind of woman he usually dated. Granted, he was very particular about whom he pursued, but his motto was always the same—no strings attached. The women knew up front what to expect, and he *always* bailed before the relationship turned demanding. One fateful night had proved he wasn't cut out for commitment and forever promises, and he wasn't willing to risk a woman's emotional stability to give any kind of long-term relationship a try.

Nope, if his own brother hadn't been able to find contentment with the one woman who embodied the perfect wife, then Marc had little hope for himself.

"Well, buddy," Ryan said, slapping him good-naturedly on the back and cutting into his thoughts. "I know finding your sister-in-law here puts a glitch in our personal plans, but we're depending on you to pull this off."

Marc lifted a brow at his friend. "After Jessica's odd brand of humor, you don't mind sharing the cabin?"

Ryan's gaze drifted toward the loft. "No doubt I'll be dodging a barrage of lawyer jokes, but I figure we'll be spending more time on the slopes than here. And if I don't find an enticing ski bunny to hook up with, I figure it's a place to sleep. It wouldn't be the first time I've crashed on the floor."

Marc glanced at Shane, who was currently flirting with Stacey as they knelt in front of the fireplace. It seemed the other man didn't have any objections to the cramped quarters, either. "I'll see what I can do."

He headed into the kitchen and found Brooke standing across the small room, near the oak table with six matching chairs—a convenient number given the current occupants of the cabin. He doubted Brooke would appreciate him using that fact as part of his argument for letting them stay.

Their gazes met, held, melded.

She folded her arms over her chest and lifted her chin, showing him the more stubborn side to her personality. Her thick, shoulder-length hair swayed with the movement, prompting him to remember the feel of his fingers tangling in those rich, luxurious, honey-blond strands as he'd angled Brooke's head for a deeper kiss. Wispy bangs touched her forehead and set off her expressive eyes, currently an intense shade of blue.

Despite her determined demeanor, her gaze revealed the wariness and caution she was really feeling. He knew those emotions were present because of the boundaries he'd unintentionally overstepped at his parents' house that night of their anniversary party.

Unfortunately, the three months that had passed since he'd last seen Brooke had done nothing to diminish the deep, sensual craving he'd developed for her. He'd tried to tell himself that moment had been instigated out of flirtatious fun, but he now had to admit that the soft, warm feel of her lips under his had seduced him, had forced him to acknowledge that flawed part of him that had coveted his brother's wife. Sweet, hot desire had gripped him, and he'd done the unthinkable and stolen a sample of what he knew would never be his—oneness, stability, eternity.

The discovery of what forever tasted like had shaken up every rule and restriction he lived by. He'd thought, he'd *hoped*, that time and distance would put their relationship back on track, as friends. He'd spent the past three months trying to get Brooke out of his mind, knowing she wasn't his kind of woman, knowing he was the last kind of man she'd go for, especially after what she'd endured with his brother. Especially when his own past track record was less than sterling.

Their time apart had only intensified their awareness of one another.

"I'm sorry, Marc," she said with an adamant shake of her head. "But having you and your friends here just isn't going to work."

He entered the room at a leisurely pace, closing the distance between them. "All of us have taken time off work until Tuesday, and there are no other lodgings available. I'm hoping we can come to some sort of compromise."

"Eric needs to hire himself a competent secretary," she muttered, more serious than joking. "We were here first, and this place isn't big enough for six. My sister and I are sharing the loft, and Stacey is taking the only other room downstairs."

"The sofa pulls out into a sleeper," he countered, stopping a safe distance away from her—for both their sakes.

She smirked, the first hint of humor dancing in her eyes. "And you and your buddies will sleep on it together?"

He visibly winced. "Uh, no. Two of us can take the floor."

"There's only one bathroom."

"That's not important to the male species," he said with a grin. "Besides, we'll be up and gone before anyone wakes up in the morning."

She released a sigh brimming with uncertainties, which he knew had to do with the subtle shift in their relationship. "Marc—"

He cut her off before she could issue an argument. "Look, Shane, Ryan and I came up here to hit the slopes, and for the most part, that's where we'll be. Or at the lodge. We just need a place to sleep at night. We'll do our own thing, and you can do yours. If you or your friends need your own time, I'm certain we can find something to do to occupy our time. In fact, we were planning on grabbing dinner at the lodge. The place will be yours tonight until nine, at least."

The determination in her gaze wavered, but then held strong, fueled by convictions only he understood.

If it was anyone but him, he knew he wouldn't be reduced to groveling.

"C'mon, Brooke," he cajoled in his best persuasive tone. "I'll talk Eric into giving you the next week that the cabin is free to make up for this fiasco."

Before she could respond, Stacey entered the kitchen. Shane followed close behind, appearing well on his way to harmony with the raven-haired beauty in front of him.

"Well?" Stacey asked impatiently. "Has the headmistress given her approval for you to stay?"

Three pairs of eyes stared at Brooke expectantly, and Marc watched her shoulders slump in defeat. "Fine, you can stay." Her tone was hardly gracious. Neither was her gaze as she leveled a pointed looked at Marc. "But no extra guests allowed. You guys are on your own for any extracurricular activities."

"Fair enough." He stifled a grin at her militant attitude. "I promise, you won't even know we're here."

BETWEEN THE HARD, carpeted floor, the chilled living room, and the erotic thoughts of the woman sleeping in the upstairs loft filtering through his mind, Marc couldn't sleep worth a damn.

Rolling to his back, he stretched his stiff muscles and cursed Ryan for drawing the longest toothpick at the Quail Valley Lodge last night, thus giving his friend the pull-out sofa bed for the night. It had been the fairest way to claim the only mattress left in the cabin, but for him and Shane who were in sleeping bags on the floor, it was hell.

Sighing, he stacked his hands beneath his head and stared up at the high-vaulted ceiling. Gradually, the first shades of dawn crept through the curtainless window, throwing shadows along the wall. He heard a rustling sound from the loft's bed, a sleepy sigh, and his gut tightened at the thought of Brooke lying in that bed, all warm and soft and sensual.

Just like she'd been when he'd kissed her. An eternity ago, it seemed, yet he could still remember every nuance of her body's response as she'd melted against him, every silky glide of their tongues, the revealing and very sexy moan that had escaped her when he'd delved even deeper, wanting more of her.

The memory prompted a slow, aching throb through his body.

He'd convinced himself that the embrace had been a fluke, a flirtatious encounter that had accidentally escalated from the kind of platonic kiss they'd shared for three years, into a swift, indulgent seduction of senses. He'd convinced himself he'd only imagined the heat and incredible need that had flared between them. He'd believed it, until he'd seen her yesterday and experienced the urge to kiss her again, to see if what they'd shared had been as explosive as he remembered.

Dangerous, crazy, insane thoughts.

He'd deliberately stayed at the lodge until after midnight, but he'd known he was in deep trouble when he couldn't summon the slightest bit of interest in the women who'd approached him, and there had been a bevy of them to choose from. While Shane and Ryan had enjoyed dancing and flirting with the female population, Marc had found himself comparing those women to Brooke...and found them all sorely lacking.

Physically, any one of them could have sufficed. Mentally, none had stimulated him beyond a token smile.

He wanted to taste Brooke again. Badly. Even though he knew he shouldn't. Knew he was completely wrong for her. And that she was completely wrong for him.

Somewhere along the way, those issues had ceased to matter.

And that's when he knew he was in big, deep trouble. The kind that tripped a guy up inside. The kind that defied logic. The kind that overruled common sense and rational judgment.

The kind that made a usually sensible, intelligent man make incredibly stupid decisions.

Ever since a relationship with a woman during his senior year in college had turned disastrous, and made Marc realize he was too much like his own father, he'd never allowed another woman to get too close emotionally—for both their sakes. The guilt that had plagued him after that incident had been excruciating. But beyond the remorse, his actions had cemented in his mind his greatest fear, that he didn't have what it took to sustain a lasting commitment—that fidelity was a chromosome missing from his family's gene pool.

For the past eight years he'd devoted his time and energy to his electrical business, and dated women who didn't make demands he knew he'd never be able to satisfy or fulfill. He'd never allowed his relationships to turn serious, and ended them before something deep and emotional developed.

One kiss, and he felt emotionally connected to

Brooke—a revelation he found both scary, and exhilarating.

Not with her, his mind chided.

Listening to the voice of reason in his head, he determined that sooner or later they needed to discuss that kiss, to put things between them back on track, and into proper perspective. They'd always been friends, and maintaining that easy, casual relationship they'd shared during her marriage to his brother was of the utmost importance to him.

With that plan firmly in mind, he unzipped his sleeping bag, got up, and made his way to the bathroom. Closing the door, he flipped on the light, and decided he'd get his shower out of the way before the women woke up and the men lost their chance at any hot water.

Half an hour later, feeling more refreshed and his aching muscles more relaxed, he slipped on a pair of long thermal underwear and shirt, and overlaid that protective warmth with jeans and a flannel shirt. Quietly exiting the bathroom, he grabbed his ski jacket and made his way to the kitchen. He found the keys for the outdoor shed on the peg by the back door.

Since it appeared his friends were sleeping off a night of too much fun, he had plenty of time to take one of the two snowmobiles parked in the shed and enjoy the light snowfall that had coated the ground during the night.

He suddenly craved something sweet. Since Brooke was out of the question, he'd just have to head down to Quail Village to the quaint bakery there and settle for confections of the pastry kind.

WHEN MARC RETURNED an hour later, the other snow-mobile was gone, the lights in the cabin were on, and the kitchen was filled with the rich aroma of freshly brewed coffee. Tugging off his gloves, he stepped into the warm kitchen and closed the door to the mudroom behind him.

Brooke and Jessica turned from the counter to face him, and he smiled. "Good morning, ladies," he greeted them, setting the pink box of pastries on the oak table.

"Morning," Brooke replied in her normal, good ol' sister-in-law tone, then turned her attention back to pouring the steaming brew into the two mugs on the counter.

Ryan walked into the kitchen, and Jessica instantly honed in on the other man. "What could be good about waking up to a lawyer trying to negotiate time in the bathroom?" she asked, stirring cream and sugar into her coffee.

A lazy smile creased Ryan's lips, and he lifted a brow over a dark brown eye glimmering with amusement. "I did *not* try and negotiate time in the bathroom."

"What was I thinking? You're absolutely right," Jessica conceded humorously. "Divorce attorneys don't know how to negotiate, they *trounce* their opponents, which is exactly what you did to me." Wandering over to the table, she peeked into the pastry box and selected a bear claw. "And just to set the record straight, Mr. Matthews, your 'I'll only be a minute' turned into twenty."

Marc met Brooke's gaze, and they both suppressed a

grin at the obvious undercurrents between the sparring couple.

Retrieving a cup from the cupboard, Ryan filled the mug with coffee. "I didn't take *that* long," he countered mildly.

Jessica crossed the room and stopped beside Ryan. "How can you tell when a lawyer is lying?" she asked sweetly, then replied before Ryan could. "His lips are moving."

With that victorious remark hanging in the air, she left the kitchen.

Marc chuckled and shook his head, feeling a twinge of sympathy for his good friend who was more used to women sweet-talking rather than mocking him.

Ryan joined him with his own deep laughter. "She's not much of a morning person, is she?"

Brooke grimaced in apology. "No, she's not."

Picking a jelly-filled doughnut from the bakery box, he took a big bite, chewing contemplatively. "You know, as crazy as it sounds, I find her very stimulating." On that note, he headed back into the living room, a grin curving his mouth and a challenging light sparking in his eyes.

As soon as Marc was alone with Brooke, silence, and a slow building awareness, settled between them. He still stood across the room, near the table, and she leaned against the far counter, looking at him over the rim of her mug as she casually sipped her coffee, but the charged energy that arced between them was unmistakable.

The instantaneous, intimate connection still startled him on an emotional level. Physically, he wasn't so surprised at his reaction. He'd always thought of Brooke as beautiful, and sensual in an understated way—her marriage to his brother hadn't blinded him to her allure. He was first and foremost a man who liked and appreciated women, and as such it was difficult not to notice the curves that made her intrinsically female—especially now, when the turtle-neck sweater she wore clung to firm breasts, and black leggings molded to the swell of her hips and those long, slender legs that had consumed too much of his thoughts lately.

But it was the warmth in her blue eyes that made his heart beat faster and caused a riot of emotions to clamor within him—wants and needs he'd denied himself for eight long years. Wants and needs he had no business contemplating now, or ever, not when he'd resigned himself to the kind of life-style that didn't include the kind of commitment a woman like Brooke demanded...and deserved.

But those sensible thoughts did nothing to douse the undeniable desire that had taken up residence in him since that kiss they'd shared. While Brooke currently displayed admirable restraint and nonchalance regarding their situation, Marc experienced a contrary surge of recklessness that battled his willpower to resist her.

Shrugging out of his jacket, Marc laid it over the back of the chair, and turned to direct his gaze at Brooke. "Got enough coffee left for me to have a cup?"

"Uh, sure," she said, a bit breathless, he suspected, from the rippling heat they'd generated in the short span of time they'd been alone.

He watched her retrieve another mug from the cupboard and pour in the last of the coffee, her hand trembling ever-so-slightly while she tried to regain her composure. Crossing the small space that separated them, he pushed his fingers through his tousled hair and away from his face, the strands still chilled from his morning ride to the village.

She turned back around, startled to find him standing beside her. With a remarkable recovery, she handed him the cup, her gaze holding his.

"You lied," she said, the accusation low and husky.

The mug stopped halfway to his lips. The very notion that he might have deceived her about something unsettled him. For all of his faults, he valued honesty, *demanded it*, in himself and others. It was a personal trait he'd insisted upon after that crisis in his life eight years ago.

"I did?" His confusion was evident in his voice.

"Yep." She nodded slowly, seriously, though there was a twinkle in her blue eyes that softened her complaint. "I thought you said you and your friends would be gone before we got up."

Relief coursed through him, and he grinned. "My intentions were honorable, I swear. But we got in after midnight, and I had no idea that the guys would be slow-moving in the morning."

She strolled over to the table and surveyed the baked goods, selecting the chocolate French cruller he'd picked specifically for her. "Wild evening at the lodge?"

"We had a good time." He took a long swallow of coffee, then shrugged, knowing he could have had a better time, if he'd been in the right frame of mind. If his mind hadn't been on Brooke. "Dinner was decent, and they've got a great band in the bar. What did you girls do last night?"

"Talked and relaxed," she said vaguely, then took a bite of her doughnut. Her eyes closed for a brief moment. Sheer enjoyment etched her features, and a tiny moan curled up from her throat.

Her tongue darted out to catch the chocolate at the side of her mouth, and he experienced an overwhelming urge to lick the icing off himself and nibble at the smear on her bottom lip.

Marc's gut clenched tight, his reserve of willpower quickly dwindling. She had no idea just how erotic she made eating a French cruller seem, and her lack of self-consciousness or inhibition made him wonder about her response in bed, beneath him, with him sliding deep inside her—

Whoa. He cut off those intimate, forbidden thoughts, but the image lingered vividly in his mind.

On a satisfied sigh, she blinked her lashes open, saw him staring at her, and a becoming shade of pink colored her cheeks.

He leaned a hip against the counter, his gaze lingering on her damp lips. "It looks good." He had firsthand knowledge that her lips, and the heated depths of her mouth, tasted equally sweet.

"It's wonderful," she admitted. "You remembered that I liked French crullers."

Lifting his gaze to her eyes, he allowed a rogue grin to grace his lips. "How can a man forget something that brings a woman such pleasure?"

The twist in his words wasn't lost on her. Her eyes widened at his sexy innuendo, but surprisingly, she made no attempt to counter his brazen comment. Finally, she drew a deep breath and looked away, breaking that irresistible, tantalizing pull.

He was flirting, crossing that invisible line he knew he ought to respect even though she was no longer married to his brother. They were both bound to get tangled up in the sensual web he was spinning if he didn't stop this madness. He tried like hell to rein himself back, to dismiss the attraction that intrigued and enticed him beyond reason or his better judgment.

He took a sip of his coffee. "You plan on skiing today?" he asked, striving for innocuous conversation.

She smiled, seemingly grateful for the change in subject. "Stacey and I are heading to the slopes in about an hour. Jessica doesn't ski, so she'll stay here." She took another bite of her doughnut, this time careful not to display her enjoyment of the pastry.

"I could give her a few basic lessons." Pushing off the counter, he slowly crossed the small space separating them. "She'd be skiing in no time."

Wariness reflected on her face as he approached, and she smoothly slipped around him and went to the sink to wash the sticky icing from her fingers. "Thanks, but I think Jessica prefers to just hang out in the cabin."

Lifting the lid on the bakery box, he grabbed a glazed buttermilk and bit into it, contemplating Brooke's sudden skittishness. "I noticed that the other snowmobile was gone. Who's using it?"

"Shane and Stacey went out for a morning ride."

"They've seemed to hit it off well," he said, guessing from the various comments Shane had made the previous night that he wouldn't mind pursuing something with the other woman. "In fact, I think my friend likes your friend."

"What's not to like?" Brooke asked, rinsing her coffee cup. "She's got a great personality, a perfect body, and she's naturally sensual."

He tilted his head, and let his gaze take stock of her attributes. "You've got a great personality, a perfect body, and you're very sensual."

She rolled her eyes at that, clearly disbelieving him.

Obviously, his brother hadn't appreciated what an enticing wife he'd had. "It's all in the eye of the beholder, I suppose." He finished off his doughnut, and sucked the glaze from his fingers, then shrugged. "I happen to think you're very sexy. Always have."

A wry grin quirked the corner of her mouth. "Interesting, considering my packaging didn't hold your brother's attention for long."

And judging by the guarded look in her eyes, she believed she couldn't hold his attention for long, either. Though his short-lived relationships verified her unspoken opinion, he found himself unjustifiably annoyed that she'd lump him into the same category as his brother.

He started toward her, and she automatically skirted to the side again, away from him and back toward the table. He turned to face her, and jammed his hands on his hips, his exasperation mounting. "You're acting as though you're afraid I'm going to pounce on you...or kiss you again."

There, he'd said it, finally brought the forbidden kiss out into the open so they could discuss it, and move on.

She seemed just as relieved to be offered an opportunity to talk about what had so obviously caused tension between them. "About that kiss—"

"Something happened between us, didn't it?" he

asked, stepping toward her from the side, so she couldn't bolt around him.

"Yes, but I think it's best if we chalk it up as a mistake." Her chin lifted as he neared. "A casual kiss that accidentally flared out of control."

Like wildfire. "No, I don't think it was a mistake or an accident," he refuted, trapping her against the solid oak table so that her bottom hit the edge. His body crowded her from the front, but didn't touch her...yet. "I think we both knew what we were doing, but then you panicked."

"I came to my senses," she argued, pressing a hand to his chest to stop him from coming any closer. One more inch and they'd be more intimate than he'd been with a woman in too many months to count. One more inch and she'd discover just how badly he wanted her, despite the dozen reasons why he shouldn't.

"Marc, this is all so complicated." She shook her head, confusion clashing with the wanting in her gaze. "If it was anyone but you..."

The honorable intentions he'd vowed earlier, to leave her alone, dissolved in that moment. Suddenly, he had a point to prove.

She gasped as his hands clasped her hips, then lifted her a fraction so her bottom slid onto the flat surface of the table. "That doesn't sound like a compliment."

She frowned at him and his bold move, but the arousing shade of her eyes contradicted her prim attitude and countered the silent reprimand in her gaze. "It wasn't meant to be a compliment, or an insult. It's the truth."

He grinned lazily and flattened his palms on her slender thighs. She sucked in a swift, shocked breath, and before she could guess his next intent, he pushed her legs apart and moved in between so her knees bracketed his hips, leaving her no possible escape.

Incredible heat shimmered between them. The initial panic touching her expression was quickly eclipsed by a thrilling rush of excitement that flowed hot and molten through Marc's veins, as well, spiraling straight toward his groin. His erection strained against thermal and denim, full and hot and heavy.

No doubt, she felt his desire and hunger for her. She swallowed convulsively. "You're my brother-in-law," she attempted.

"Ex," he breathed, dipping his head near her ear, squashing her paltry argument. Before she could issue a more obvious objection, that he was a *Jamison*, he distracted her by sliding his lips against the silken skin of her neck. "I haven't been able to get you out of my mind since that kiss."

A tiny moan caught in her throat, and she gripped the edge of the table with her fingers, seemingly trying desperately to resist him. "Me, either," she admitted, sounding miserable.

He slid his hand to the nape of her neck, curling his fingers just beneath the French braid she'd twisted her hair into. He touched his lips to her jaw, dragged them to the corner of her mouth, which was parted and trembling. He lifted his head, just enough to look into her soft blue eyes, brimming with anticipation, despite her protests.

That was the only assurance he needed to take this encounter to the next level. "You're curious," he murmured huskily, "I'm tempted, we both want it, so let's try another kiss and see what's really there."

She shuddered, resisting, her body stiff with tension. He waited for her to give him the permission he sought, because this time he wasn't about to take something she wasn't willing to give.

This time, he wanted no regrets, no excuses.

Through half-mast lashes, he watched her struggle with her conscience, and prepared to let her and this fleeting moment go—probably the smartest thing for him to do.

He started to step back, but she suddenly reached out and gripped his flannel shirt in her hands, pulling him back—close. Determination fired her blue eyes, and she drew a deep, fortifying breath.

"Just do it," she ordered.

3

MARC BLINKED, surprise registering in his gaze at Brooke's ardent demand. "Excuse me?"

Brooke dampened her bottom lip with her tongue. Her heart pounded frantically in her chest, and her entire body was charged with a nervousness she couldn't deny. "Just do it!" *Before I change my mind*, she thought desperately.

He tilted his head, a curious smile canting the corner of that sensual mouth she knew was capable of giving her great pleasure. "Demanding thing, aren't you?" he murmured.

He had no idea. Right now, she didn't want to think about what she was about to do, or her reckless, irresponsible behavior, or the excitement spiraling low in her belly. She had a point to demonstrate, to him and herself...that she *could* just do it.

Forcing herself to be the aggressor, she released her grip on his flannel shirt and slid her palm around to the nape of his neck. Her fingers glided through the silky length of his black-as-midnight hair. The strands were cool, contrasting with the fevered heat radiating from his body and the smoldering intensity darkening his eyes.

She shivered, and before she came to her senses, she pulled his mouth toward hers. His head dipped willingly, without hesitation, and his soft, warm lips settled over hers with a gentleness that threw her plan for a mindless seduction off-kilter. She'd wanted, *expected*, fast, wild and unemotional. He gave her slow, lazy and tantalizing, catering to her doubts and uncertainties...and the tension thrumming through her.

His large hands stroked down her back, encouraging her closer, making her spine arch until her breasts brushed his wide, hard chest. The delicious friction caused her nipples to tighten and ache. He gripped her hips and slowly pulled her bottom to the very edge of the table, spreading her legs wider and pressing against her until the only thing separating them was heavy denim and cotton leggings.

He sucked her bottom lip into his mouth, nibbled on the soft flesh with his teeth, and a moan slipped past her throat before she could catch it. Her mind spun, and her thighs clenched against his lean hips.

"You need to relax," he murmured against her mouth. She felt her lips gradually soften and part for him. "Yeah, that's it," he said, then exerted a more provocative pressure with his mouth. "Now give me your tongue..."

Shivering at the husky, rich tone of his voice, she did as he ordered. Completely meshing their lips, she slid her tongue into his mouth and instantly tangled with his, silky slow and lush with promise. The flavor of hot male and honey glaze from the doughnut he'd eaten overwhelmed her, excited her, and made her melt and relax against him.

Three months ago the kiss they'd shared had been a thrill ride neither one of them had expected, giving them little time to explore and enjoy taste and textures.

This time, he was entirely too thorough, incredibly indulgent, and generous in catering to her pleasure.

This languorous kiss, as titillating as it was, suddenly wasn't enough. The need to be a little bit wild and a whole lot uninhibited swept through her. Framing his jaw in her hands, she opened her mouth wider beneath his and took control before she came to her reliable, responsible senses. The pace of their kiss immediately quickened, grew wetter and deeper and shockingly suggestive as their tongues entwined and stroked and mated.

Amazed that she could feel so physically needy, so intensely aroused so quickly, she gave into the sensations lapping at her feminine nerves, screaming for a more sexually charged contact. Locking her calves at the back of Marc's muscular thighs, she pulled him even closer, welcoming the heat and pressure of him against her newly aroused, swollen flesh.

Marc groaned deep in his throat, the sound reverberating against her lips, her breasts, her belly, *between her thighs*. Unable to help herself, she tilted her hips and deliberately rubbed against the hard ridge straining the fly of his jeans. She rubbed sinuously again and gasped as he instinctively pushed back, a slow, purposeful stroke that seemed as intimate as him being inside her.

That shameless friction triggered a rush of dampness, a deep clenching of her body, and stole her breath. Their hot, openmouthed kiss turned ravenous and urgent, and he did it again, sliding rhythmically against her, as if he couldn't help himself.

Desire rippled through her, coiling tight in her belly. An explosive, wondrous climax beckoned, and she whimpered, struggling between holding on and letting go of those restrictions and good-girl tendencies that had ruled her life for so many years.

And just like the first time they'd kissed, she came to her senses and *panicked*. Physically, he thrilled her, turning her on faster than any man ever had. But it was the complex emotions he evoked that threw off her balance.

The sound of the snowmobiles approaching the cabin escalated Brooke's alarm. Wedging her hands between them, she pushed her palms against his shoulders frantically, and he immediately came to his senses and pulled away.

Stumbling back, Marc plopped down in the nearest chair, looking dazed and undeniably aroused. "Wow," he murmured, scrubbing a hand over his jaw. "That was incredible."

Scrambling down from the table, Brooke pressed her palms to her flaming cheeks, unable to deny his claim. Her body buzzed with unfulfilled desire, throbbing for the climax that had been so, so close. She'd been so primed he could have taken her on the table—and how would she have explained her torrid embrace to her sister, who was only a room away? No doubt Jessica would call her a fool for getting involved with another Jamison, for allowing hormones to reduce her to a mass of nerves and sensations with only a need for ultimate satisfaction on her mind.

What made her believe she could indulge in a mindblowing kiss with him and not want more?

She shook her head, afraid to think of what might happen with all that volatile passion if they ever made love. Not that she was contemplating getting naked with him! "Marc, we can't do this."

"I know," he agreed, his voice tight and strained. He shifted in his chair to find a more comfortable position. Clearly unable to accommodate the bulge straining the zipper of his jeans, he instead clasped his hands strategically in his lap.

She straightened her sweater with a yank, and nearly groaned as the rasping sensation tantalized her sensitive nipples. "Well, don't worry, it won't happen again."

His gaze narrowed perceptively, a spark of Jamison challenge glimmering in his eyes, as if she'd issued him a dare. "You don't think so?"

"I *know* so," she said adamantly.

The sound of Shane's deep voice and Stacey's flirtatious laughter drifted from just outside the kitchen door leading to the back area of the cabin. Brooke willed the couple inside, fervently hoping they'd interrupt what had become a very awkward conversation.

Marc glanced at the door, then back at her, knowing his time was limited. "Brooke, two people don't kiss like that unless there's a certain chemistry and a strong attraction between them."

One she couldn't afford to explore further. Not with him. "Call it a release of sexual frustration. It's been a long, celibate year for me."

Irritation creased his expression at her flippant tone. "So you're insinuating that you would have responded to *any* man the same way?"

No, she thought miserably, knowing that a faceless stranger wouldn't have evoked such a startling heat, hunger and *need*. But that was part of the problem with

Marc. She'd never responded so shamelessly, so eagerly to a man in her entire life. Neither Eric nor her one sexual encounter in college had prepared her for this. Marc's magnetism and appeal seemed to strip away every proper, responsible characteristic she'd honed since the age of thirteen, reducing her to a sensual creature who couldn't get enough of that blend of excitement and ecstasy Marc's kisses promised.

She shrugged indifferently, letting the gesture speak for itself, since she couldn't bring herself to lie to him.

His lips at first pursed, then he opened his mouth to argue—just as the back door opened and Stacey and Shane entered the kitchen, thankfully intercepting his rebuttal.

"That morning ride was incredibly exhilarating!" Stacey said, sounding like a giddy schoolgirl in the throes of her first crush.

Ignoring the extra occupants in the room, Marc swallowed back whatever words he'd been about to impart, but boldly held Brooke's gaze. Indeed, she couldn't look away. Through the slight haze of frustration and confusion, his eyes conveyed a startling message—they weren't finished with this particular issue. And he wasn't finished with her.

The silent claim he staked caused Brooke's internal temperature to spike, despite the gust of cool air Shane and Stacey's arrival had invited into the room. Her traitorous pulse fluttered, stoking the desire simmering just beneath the surface. Did she even stand a chance if Marc followed through with that sexy threat to pursue her?

"Umm, are we interrupting something?" Stacey asked, too much interest infusing her voice.

The last thing Brooke wanted was Stacey speculating over her relationship with Marc, and coming to conclusions she didn't want to discuss with a woman who had a fearless, fabulous sex life.

Before she could formulate a response, Marc stood, the evidence of what had transpired between them earlier not nearly as obvious now that his body and libido had time to cool. "You're not interrupting anything that Brooke and I can't resolve at another time." Though he answered Stacey, his gaze never wavered from Brooke's.

In her opinion, there was nothing left for them to resolve. Of course the rogue knew she wouldn't oppose him with an audience listening in on their debate.

Finally, he glanced at Shane. "You ready to head over to the lodge for the day?"

Shane exchanged a reluctant look with Stacey that made it clear they would have preferred to spend the day together. "Yeah, I'm ready."

Stacey winked at Shane as she casually pulled off her lined gloves. "I'll catch up with you on the slopes later," she promised.

The two men left the kitchen, and an unnerving silence settled over the room.

Stacey unwrapped the colorful scarf from her neck, a knowing smile curving lips stung red from the cold. "Well, well, well," she murmured.

Brooke knew exactly what those three simple words meant, knew precisely what was tumbling through Stacey's mind. She held up a hand to ward off her friend's interrogation. "I don't want to talk about it."

"All right," Stacey conceded, but her gaze sparkled

with mischief and a wicked provocation. "You ready to put last night's plan into action?"

No. Without the buzz of the margarita giving her courage and with the taste of Marc still lingering on her tongue, going out on a man-hunt held little appeal. But she desperately needed the distraction, and there was always the possibility that flirting with another man, and enjoying his attentions, would make her forget about Marc and that luscious, earth-shattering kiss they shared.

Pulling in a deep breath, she fabricated an optimistic smile. "I'm ready. Let's do it."

STACEY NUDGED BROOKE with her elbow and gestured to a good-looking blond-haired guy making his way to the end of the line for the ski lift, where the two of them were waiting their turn.

"What do you think of him?" Stacey asked out of the corner of her mouth. "He has a great body, and a nice smile."

Brooke tried to regard her friend's newest quarry objectively, and like every other man Stacey had singled out, she found herself comparing him to Marc, whose body proved to be a perfect fit for hers, and who owned a lazy smile that seemed to stroke her senses as intimately as a caress. This guy's physique didn't spark even a glimmer of interest, and his smile was a shade too cocky for her liking. And she was coming to realize that she preferred dark hair over light.

A curvaceous woman crossed the man's path. Without an ounce of subtlety, he craned his neck around and lowered his sunglasses to gawk at her retreating backside, a wolfish smile transforming his features.

Brooke rolled her eyes, completely turned off by the guy's arrogance and playboy image. "He looks like he's on the prowl."

Amused laughter bubbled out of Stacey as they moved closer to the head of the line. "Oh, and we aren't?" she asked wryly. "I thought finding a man for you was the purpose of today's expedition."

"It was. I mean, it *is*," she amended, trying to sound enthusiastic. "I just haven't seen a guy yet that makes me want to tap into that wild side you're so sure I'm suppressing."

The ski lift attendant motioned them into position, and both she and Stacey held tight to their poles as the next chair swung around, swooped them up, and began its ascent to the top of the intermediate slope.

"You've rejected about a dozen prospects so far just at a glance, without giving any of them a fair chance," Stacey said, continuing their conversation without missing a beat. "There are only so many single men on the mountain, Brooke, and you've narrowed the field considerably."

Brooke made a playful face at her friend. "The day is young, and we still have all afternoon." She shrugged. "I don't want to 'settle.'"

A sudden, dreamy sigh drifted from Stacey. "I, personally, would settle for Shane, and be perfectly happy for the rest of our vacation."

"I think the feeling is mutual." Brooke grinned at Stacey's obvious intentions. "I take it you're going to 'just do it' with Shane?"

"Oh, yeah." Stacey waggled her brows lasciviously. "The first chance we get."

Brooke chuckled and shook her head. Glad that

she'd managed to reroute Stacey's thought process, she glanced down at the crowd of people below enjoying the recent snowfall, and promptly frowned when she caught sight of Marc at the base of the beginner's slope. He was hard to miss, with his shock of thick black hair, those wide shoulders she'd clung to this morning, and black Lycra coveralls that defined his lean, honed body and sexy male attributes.

He was helping a little girl about the age of eight learn to ski, and alternating his attention to the very grown woman accompanying the child. The redhead appeared completely captivated with Marc and had no qualms about touching him at every opportunity.

She released a disgruntled snort that did little to alleviate the growing pressure in her chest. Their kiss wasn't even cold and Marc was already moving on to another more willing female. As the lift climbed higher, she twisted around to keep him in sight, disgusted with her weakness for yet another Jamison. And she fiercely resented that the lusty embrace they'd shared in the kitchen had meant very little to Marc, while her body was still trying to deal with the shimmering after-effects of that encounter.

"For crying out loud, Brooke, I can't take this anymore."

Stacey's exasperated tone had Brooke straightening in her seat so fast she nearly gave herself whiplash. The carriage rocked precariously, and Brooke gripped the safety bar for support. "You can't take what anymore?" She blinked in wide-eyed innocence at Stacey.

Her friend raised a perfectly arched brow. "What's going on between you and Marc?"

"*Nothing*," she said, then winced at the too-adamant

tone of her voice, as if she were trying to convince herself of the fact.

Stacey scoffed. "Yeah, right. There were enough sparks in the kitchen this morning to light up the sky on the Fourth of July." A humorous smile curled the corners of her mouth. "Maybe you don't need to look any further than our own cabin for your *prospect*."

"Are you nuts?" Her high-pitched voice echoed in the high altitude, and she lowered her volume when she realized she'd garnered the attention of the couple ahead of them. "Marc is my brother-in-law!"

"Ex," Stacey reminded her oh-so-helpfully, making the excuse a flimsy one. "Which makes him just as eligible for your vacation fling as any other man in Quail Valley."

Brooke sucked cold mountain air into her lungs, which only served to make her light-headed. "Except for the fact that he's not a stranger I can just leave behind." She had a feeling if she sampled a taste of mindless sexual gratification with Marc there would be no going back, that she'd want more than he was capable of giving—like sentimental desires and expectations. She wasn't willing to risk the staid, orderly existence she'd adopted after her divorce for that kind of emotional upheaval.

The chair headed toward their drop-off, and Stacey flipped up the fur-lined collar of her jacket around her neck while slanting Brooke a mocking look. "Jeez, it was just a suggestion. You don't have to get so defensive."

"I'm not getting defensive," she argued, then immediately softened her tone. "I'm trying to be reasonable."

"I thought we agreed that was part of your problem, that you're way too analytical and pragmatic." She tugged on her gloves, and gripped her ski poles in her right hand in anticipation of exiting the lift. "Judging by that flush I saw on your face this morning in the kitchen, I'm guessing that Marc turned you on."

Brooke's cheeks burned, and it had nothing to do with the cold or stinging breeze, and everything to do with Stacey's accurate summary of her morning episode with Marc. She didn't bother issuing a futile denial when the truth remained, that she was *still* turned on.

Stacey grinned in her own personal victory. "Why pursue some stranger if the guy who turns you on is standing right in front of you?" Having imparted those pearls of wisdom, Stacey released the safety bar and glanced at her one last time. "Now, if you don't mind, I've got my own prospect to pursue."

Brooke slipped her sunglasses back on to cut the glare from the sun and snow. "Shane doesn't stand a chance."

Stacey's laugh was throaty and very confident. "Of course he doesn't. Ta-ta for now." And then she was off.

Brooke hopped down from the lift after Stacey and skied down the slope at a leisurely pace. By the time she reached the base, Marc and the redhead were nowhere to be found. Brooke wasn't surprised. Attempting to put him out of her mind, she forced herself to enjoy the great skiing conditions and exercise.

The afternoon passed quickly. At a quarter after three Brooke decided on one last run before heading to the lodge for a latte, and to wait for Stacey so they could head back to the cabin. She trudged toward the ski lift line to wait her turn.

"Mind if I share a chair with you?"

Every nerve ending tingled to life at the deep, masculine timbre of Marc's voice. She glanced over her shoulder and found the object of her fantasies standing there with an adorable grin tipping the corners of his mouth. He wore reflective sunglasses, and she disliked being at a disadvantage, unable to read that bold gaze of his.

She gave an indifferent shrug, though she was feeling anything but. "No, I don't mind."

Once they were situated on the lift and the chair began its climb skyward, Brooke slanted him a casual glance. "Did things not work out with the redhead?" she asked, and immediately chastised herself for being so blunt.

Finally, he removed that barrier in front of his expressive eyes, letting the nylon cord around his neck catch the sunglasses as they dropped against his chest. Tilting his head, his brows puckered thoughtfully. "The redhead?"

As if he didn't know who she was talking about! "The one with the little girl."

Understanding dawned, and the knowing grin spreading across his handsome face crinkled the skin at the corners of his eyes. "Ahh, the *redhead*."

Brooke bit the inside of her cheek, too affected by the teasing glint in his smoky-gray eyes. Despite herself, she marveled that Marc was so different in personality from his older, more serious brother—so fun-loving, carefree and playful. But there was one similarity the two brothers shared, a significant characteristic she couldn't discount. "You move on quick, Jamison."

Stretching his arm across the back of the chair, he touched his gloved fingers to her jaw, his bemusement fading into something far more resolute and sincere. "And you're jumping to wrong conclusions, honey."

A head-to-toe shiver coursed through her. It had nothing to do with the cold weather, but was provoked by the rumbly sound of his voice, the heat in his gaze, and the raspy feel of his glove against her skin. *Honey.* The endearment was intimate and personal, a pet name even Eric hadn't used with her. It made her feel special and cherished and too close to falling for Marc's innate charm.

Trying not to let his sweet-talk distract her, she responded to his statement with a challenge of her own—even as her mind whispered that she shouldn't care what his intentions with the redhead had been. Unfortunately, their kiss had struck a possessive bone in her body she hadn't known existed. "Am I jumping to the wrong conclusion?"

"Yeah, you are." He held her gaze, his eyes clear and honest, offering her something Eric never had—a keen sense of trust. "I know how it probably looked, but I was teaching the little girl to ski. She'd taken a couple of hard spills and was crying because she was frustrated, and I didn't want her to give up when I knew once she got the hang of it she'd have a blast."

"Ahh," she murmured, striving for a humorous note. "A very clever way to get to know her mother better."

He laughed, the rich, unfettered sound wrapping around Brooke like a warm, fuzzy blanket on a chilly day. "Oh, the woman was definitely interested, but I wasn't. But don't worry, I let her down gently." He blinked those long, sooty lashes of his lazily. "I spent about an hour with Amber, showing her the basic moves, and before long she was mastering the bunny slope and I had a line of about half a dozen other kids begging for lessons."

"So you spent the afternoon teaching kids how to ski?" She couldn't keep the incredulity from her voice.

"Pretty much." He gave her French braid a gentle tug. "Don't look so shocked. I enjoy kids."

Brooke pictured the scene, with Marc surrounded by six or more eager children, all vying for his attention. Judging by the wide grin on his face, he'd reveled in playing ski instructor to the little imps.

"I have to admit that I *am* surprised. Eric was never really comfortable around children."

Marc's lips thinned. Obviously, the comparison didn't please or flatter him in the least. "And you just automatically assumed the same applied for me?"

She glanced away, toward the approaching unloading station, ashamed to admit that she'd done exactly that—unfairly painting Marc with the same brush as Eric when there was so much she didn't know about Marc. She owed him an apology.

Meeting his troubled gaze, and wondering about the emotions swirling in the shadowed depths, she attempted to explain. "I'm sorry—"

"I don't claim to be perfect, Brooke," he cut in quickly, seeming to want to state his own argument before they reached the ramp and he lost the opportunity. "I've made mistakes I'm not proud of, but I'd like to think that I've learned from them. I just want you to know that what you see is exactly what you get. I don't pretend to be anything more or less."

Brooke swallowed, hard. What she saw was someone who was caring and *honest*, a trait she'd learned to value above all else at a very early age. A quality she'd realized too late had been absent in her marriage to Eric. She appreciated that characteristic in Marc, along with his ability to speak openly and candidly without fearing what others might think. She was learning that he was a man who didn't hide behind pretenses...as his brother had.

The chair made the connection into the station and the safety bar unlatched under the pressure of Marc's gloved hand. He glanced at her one last time and flashed her a quick smile that dissolved the serious moment and put their relationship back into familiar territory—as friends.

"Thanks for the ride." Slipping on his glasses, he moved to the edge of his seat until his skis skimmed hard-packed snow. "I'll see you back at the cabin."

She watched him go, then followed behind. While Marc navigated the hill with finesse and speed, Brooke opted to take her last ride down the slope slow and easy.

What you see is exactly what you get. Marc's comment echoed in her mind, along with Stacey's remark about him being a suitable prospect. The two went hand in hand, she realized with sudden insight.

She'd automatically discounted the idea of having a wild fling with Marc as ludicrous, but now she reconsidered that option. He might not be a stranger she could leave behind, but he was a man who wouldn't expect anything more from her than the good time she was determined to have before returning to her dependable job and her responsible, *boring* life. Separating her feelings for Marc from her quest for physical gratification wouldn't be easy, but she was determined to have this, and him, and for once in her life ignore her practical, sensible nature.

Their undeniable attraction was a bonus, and they'd proved with two kisses that the chemistry between them would be explosive. Awesomely so. She didn't doubt that he'd be an attentive, focused lover...and she could depend on him to keep their liaison discreet.

A slow smile curved her mouth. He *was* the perfect candidate. She knew and trusted him, which made more sense than taking a risk with someone she truly didn't know. She and Marc were beyond first kisses, so there would be no awkward moments to worry about, no wondering if *she* turned *him* on. She already knew.

Oh, yeah, she thought with a renewed surge of excitement. If she indulged in all Marc had to offer without any expectations besides pleasure and fun, she'd walk away satisfied and Marc would have enjoyed the challenge—a win-win situation.

She wanted this. For once, she wanted to please *herself*, without analyzing the outcome or worrying about consequences. She wanted to shuck her reserved, practical nature, forget insecurities, and experience lust and passion in its fullest measure. Marc had given her a taste of that particular ecstasy, and she was determined to devour the entire sensual feast.

Only one issue stood in her way...figuring out a way to proposition Marc.

4

MARC TOOK A SEAT across from Ryan in the cabin's living room and glanced at his friend's swollen foot, which was propped up on the coffee table. "Hey, buddy, how's the ankle doing?"

Ryan shrugged and settled himself more comfortably on the sofa cushion, wincing as the movement jarred his injury. "Okay, but I'm still ticked off at that jerk who cut me off," he grumbled. "I'm pretty sure it's nothing more serious than a slight sprain."

Jessica entered the living room from the kitchen on the tail end of Ryan's comment, holding a bag of ice. "Slight?" she repeated, then rolled her eyes incredulously. "You'd think he'd had his leg amputated by the way he's been complaining and acting completely helpless."

Marc hid a grin, suspecting Ryan's helpless act was strictly for Jessica's benefit. No doubt, he was playing up his injury in hopes of gaining some attention and feminine sympathy, and surprisingly, his ploy had worked to a small degree. "Well, it's nice of you to help him out."

Jessica bent over and arranged the makeshift cold compress on the puffy, purplish skin around Ryan's ankle. "I was passing through the living room and he caught me at a weak moment."

Ryan eyed Jessica's curvaceous backside apprecia-tively. "Yeah, I'm feeling really weak, and a little fever-ish, too."

Straightening, Jessica cast Ryan a guileless smile that belied the sassy glint in her gaze. "I'd be happy to get you another ice pack...for your lap."

Shane, who sat on the opposite end of the couch from Ryan, chuckled. As soon as Jessica disappeared into the kitchen again, he addressed Ryan. "You asked for that, Matthews."

"She wants me," Ryan responded confidently. "And it's gonna take a whole lot more than a bag of ice to cool me off where she's concerned."

Marc leaned back in his seat, silently echoing Ryan's sentiment as it pertained to Brooke and himself. Ever since that morning's sexy kiss he'd been feeling hot and bothered, and more than a little restless. The first kiss they'd shared had been a shocking revelation. Their second had been explosive and beyond anything in his experience. The emotional fallout had left him reeling, and completely tied up in knots.

He wanted Brooke more than he'd ever wanted an-other woman. His need for her was basic and elemen-tal, yet he was smart enough to know that a relation-ship with her was way too complicated to consider— because of her past with his brother, and his own past mistake that kept him from committing to any one woman.

For longer than he cared to recall he'd harbored a se-cret attraction toward Brooke. All through her mar-riage to Eric he'd kept their relationship friendly, flir-tatious, and not too personal, infinitely careful not to cross those matrimonial boundaries. Now, he had an overwhelming urge to discover her as a woman, to tap into the thoughts that filled her head, and explore the full extent of their compatibility in bed.

Dangerous, insane, *impossible* thoughts. Yet that knowledge didn't stop him from fantasizing about her, and them, and spinning numerous "what if" scenarios that made him feel hotter than he'd been as a teenager.

Female voices from the loft captured Marc's attention and drew his gaze to Brooke and Stacey as they descended the stairs to the lower level of the cabin. He and Brooke hadn't talked since their conversation on the lift, and as their eyes made contact he detected something different about her.

He'd expected polite reserve and a whole lot of distance after his honest, "what you see is what you get" spiel. Yet she exuded a new kind of confidence in the smile lifting the corners of her lush mouth and in the easy, sensual way she moved. The sway of her slender hips mesmerized him, her lithe legs encased in those form-fitting leggings provoked wicked, sinful thoughts that, unfortunately, would never play out in real life.

"So, what do you think, Marc, do you still want to grab dinner at the lodge?" Shane asked.

Marc blinked and transferred his gaze to his friends. "Are you okay with that, Ryan?"

"Hey, don't let me stop the two of you from having a good time," he replied sincerely. "I'll be fine."

"Grabbing dinner at the lodge sounds good to me," Marc agreed, figuring he'd be better off in a crowd of people than alone with Brooke in this tiny cabin. "And since there are only two of us going, we can take the snowmobiles."

"Sounds like fun," Stacey said as she and Brooke strolled over to the couches, just as Jessica exited the kitchen with a mug of hot tea. "Brooke and I were just talking about heading to the lodge for dinner, too, and maybe some dancing afterward. Would you two mind if we hitched a ride on the snowmobiles?"

"Not at all," Shane replied quickly, his tone as enthusiastic as his smile.

Marc fully expected Brooke to balk at the bold way her friend invited them along, and the obvious fact that she'd be partnered with him for the ride. But again, that new poise and self-assurance presented itself, making him wonder what she was up to.

Brooke cast a concerned look her sister's way. "Are you okay with me going to the lodge for the evening, Jess?" she asked, her insinuation clear. With the four of them gone, Jessica would be alone with Ryan.

Jessica took a sip of her tea, her eyes gleaming mischievously over the rim of her mug as she considered the question. "No, I don't mind," she said after a moment. "I kinda like the thought of having a crippled lawyer at my mercy."

Ryan groaned good-naturedly. "Go easy on me, sweetheart."

"See, he's already pleading for deliverance," she quipped, a triumphant smile curving her mouth. "Don't worry about us, we'll get along *just* fine."

Twenty minutes later, the four of them were dressed in their snowsuits over their regular clothing to keep warm during their ride to the lodge. Outside, they paired up to each snowmobile.

"See you there," Stacey called out and waved back at Marc and Brooke before wrapping her arms securely around Shane's waist. The snowmobile's engine rumbled, and then they drove off with the illumination of the full moon leading the way.

Brooke watched them go, then glanced up at the night sky. "Looks like there are some heavy clouds moving in," she commented, tugging on her gloves. "Have you heard what the weather is supposed to be like for the next few days?"

"Nope." Marc sat astride the long seat and slipped his insulated helmet over his head. "When I come up to the mountains, I try to leave all aspects of civilization behind, including radios and TVs. As far as the weather is concerned, I just go with the flow and hope for lots of fresh snow."

She approached the snowmobile, a wry smile on her lips as she buckled her helmet strap beneath her chin, leaving the face shield open. "If you claim to leave civilization behind, what excuse do you have for the cell phone I've seen you talking on a few times since you've been here?"

He absently patted his jacket, checking for the compact phone he kept tucked inside the breast pocket. "That's one thing I don't leave home without. I'm up here to relax, play and have a good time, but bottom line, I've got a business to run and I like to stay in touch with my secretary, and my foremen."

He slapped his gloved hand to the space behind him, beckoning her with a lazy smile. "Hop on."

The Brooke he knew would have scrutinized the situation, deemed the proximity of their bodies too intimate, and possibly bowed out at the last minute with a convenient excuse. Without delays or the uncertainties he'd come to associate with Brooke when it came to *them*, she straddled the leather seat behind him. Her spread thighs bracketed his, and her pelvis cradled his bottom with snug precision.

Gulping cold air, he turned on the engine and let it idle and warm while marveling at her daring demeanor. He had no idea where or when the transformation had occurred, but he couldn't deny that Brooke's newfound confidence and sensuality tightened his gut and made resisting her difficult as hell.

It also made him want to see just how far she was willing to go with her blossoming, sexy, arousing attitude. The challenge was too appealing to pass up. He revved the engine, making the seat beneath them vibrate as the RPMs climbed, then turned his head to the side so she could hear him. "What kind of ride are you looking for? You want to take it slow and easy, or do you want it fast and wild?"

The question startled her—the slight stiffening of her body gave her away—but she recovered quickly. She leaned forward, so that her chest pressed against his back and the sides of their helmets touched. "If you think you can keep it up, I'll take it fast and wild." Her breath was so warm, the night so cold, that her breath evaporated in a puff of white that seemed to glow in the darkness.

He chuckled, enjoying their sexy banter too much. "I've never had a problem keeping it up before." He switched on the headlamp and tossed out a last safety precaution. "Hold on tight, honey, and get ready for the ride of your life."

She did as he instructed, wrapping her arms around him and aligning their bodies from shoulders to knees. Her arms rested low on his hips, and her gloved and entwined fingers settled in his lap. His clothing was layered, but even through thermal, denim and the insulated down of his snowsuit pants he could feel the tantalizing pressure of her hands.

In an effort to cool his response, he took off toward the lodge, giving Brooke the thrill ride he'd promised her. He hit every slope on the way, making her squeal in a combination of delight and fear. They arrived at their destination almost half an hour later because he'd played along the way, laughing and breathless, and Marc felt more in control of his libido.

He planned to keep things that way for the evening, even if being chivalrous killed him. For as much as Brooke was sending off those sensual, flirtatious signals, for as much as he wanted to give free license to that mutual attraction and desire, he knew too much about regrets to take advantage of what she was subtly intimating. He wasn't about to compound the guilt he carried by adding Brooke to his unrelenting conscience.

He parked the snowmobile in the designated area, and they met up with Stacey and Shane just inside the lobby of the lodge. The heat inside engulfed them, warming their faces and thawing cold body parts.

Men's and women's changing areas and locker rooms flanked the long ticket desk in the lobby, and Marc deliberately headed toward the men's room while unzipping his jacket, forcing Shane to follow. The women automatically drifted to their side, too.

"We'll see you two around the fire pit in the bar after dinner," Marc said, effectively establishing the distance he needed between him and Brooke, while Sta-

cey and Shane exchanged a look that promised they'd
meet up with one another later.

But it was the disappointment he saw in Brooke's
gaze that made him feel like a heel. Telling himself he
was doing them both a big favor by not pursuing what
she was inviting did nothing to ease his conscience, or
his need for her.

HOW WAS SHE supposed to seduce Marc when another
woman had gotten to him first and was busy attempting the same thing?

Brooke tried not to glare at the pretty blonde bestow-
ing a dazzling smile upon Marc as the two of them engaged in a conversation at the bar in the lounge. Instead, she wrapped her fingers around her mug of Irish
coffee and took a drink. Warm liquid settled in her
belly, and only seemed to stoke the flames of jealousy
flickering inside her.

She shook her head at that thought—she'd never
been the possessive sort and was more than a little disgruntled that Marc was the one to evoke such a covet-
ous emotion. And twice in one day!

Even with Eric she'd maintained a level head and
sensible attitude about his indiscretions. She hadn't
ranted, raved, or made an ugly scene when he'd con-
fessed, just calmly came to the realization that their
marriage had been based on false expectations on both
of their parts, and that neither one of them had been
able to live up to the other's high hopes.

Now that she'd had time to analyze the situation,
she'd come to the conclusion that an emotional connection had been lacking in her relationship with Eric.
From the beginning they'd been friends. Gradually,

they'd become lovers, and from there, they'd each stepped into their role as husband and wife. Despite all that, they'd never shared all the intimacies that most married couples did. Passion hadn't been a part of their union, either. Their relationship had been superficial, with no real substance to hold it together.

She'd fallen for Eric's charm and pursuit and expected a lasting marriage, a house in the suburbs and strong family values that they'd pass on to their children. As for Eric, he'd attempted to deny his playboy tendencies behind the pretense of marriage, but in the end his true nature had prevailed and he'd admitted that he couldn't suppress the urge to be with other women.

They'd opted for divorce, and she'd parted ways with Eric experiencing more disappointment than resentment over the end to their marriage. It had been a mistake, on both their parts. She'd accepted that and was ready to move on to the next phase of her life.

And that phase included seducing the sexy, good-looking man who made her pulse race with desire. Except Marc had his own agenda tonight, which didn't include flirting with *her*.

Sighing, she found Stacey and Shane out on the dance floor having a good time together. At least Stacey had landed *her* man, Brooke thought with a small smile. She saw the blonde at the bar grasp Marc's hand and laughingly insist he dance with her. When he obliged, Brooke decided it was time that she did the same and accepted the invitations of the men she'd been turning down for the past half hour.

Unfortunately, she couldn't drum up any enthusiasm for her partners beyond mild interest. None made her feel desirable or caused that undeniable feminine reaction Marc could elicit with just a grin. There was no instantaneous attraction, no sizzling awareness. No excitement or sexy thrill just by looking into their eyes. Every one of those responses was reserved for the gorgeous bad boy who'd offered her a few token smiles from across the lounge in the past hour.

"Hey, folks," the band's lead singer cut in after the song had ended, garnering everyone's attention. "An emergency weather report just came in and it seems we have a blizzard heading our way and we're going to be in for white-out conditions, possibly through tomorrow. We'll be closing the lodge early so our employees can make it home safely. I suggest you all do the same."

Everyone took the weather report seriously, and the crowd in the bar area immediately dispersed and thinned. Stacey had informed Brooke twenty minutes ago that she and Shane were heading back to the cabin to take advantage of the Jacuzzi, so that left her and Marc to follow behind on their own.

She spotted Marc across the room talking to the blonde, who pouted in disappointment over whatever he was saying. Brooke imagined Marc regretted bringing her along on the snowmobile, which put a definite crimp in any evening plans he might have entertained with the other woman.

After a moment, he strolled over to her, parting ways with the blonde. "You ready to go?" he asked.

She slanted him a meaningful glance, while squashing that green-eyed monster swirling within her. "You know, I'm more than capable of taking the snowmobile back to the cabin by myself if you'd like to spend your evening elsewhere."

He smiled and lightly grasped her elbow as he ushered her toward the lockers. "I'm not going to let you out there on your own with a blizzard heading in."

Concern for her welfare. Nothing more. His indifference toward her the past few hours nipped at her, provoking her, making her irritable and frustrated on too many levels.

By the time they were bundled up in their snowsuits and headed outside, the winds had kicked up and fat flurries were falling. The full moon that had guided them earlier was now covered by dark, menacing clouds. Even the temperature felt as though it had dipped drastically in the few hours they'd been at the lodge. As she trudged behind Marc, the fierce winds stung her cheeks, a warning of more temperamental weather to come.

"It doesn't look like we have a whole lot of time before the brunt of the blizzard hits," she called out to him as she took her place behind him on the leather seat.

He turned his head so she could hear his reply. "I know a short cut. We'll be back at the cabin in no time at all."

She opened her mouth to tell him that she thought they should stick to the familiar trail, but decided against arguing. All she wanted was to get back to the cabin so she could head up to the loft and wallow in her failed attempt to seduce Marc. The sooner they arrived, the better.

She held on as he took off, but this ride lacked the fun and excitement the first one had. There were no sexy innuendos, no laughter, just a straight trek through territory she didn't recognize. The swirl of snow from the oncoming storm reduced their vision and slowed their speed considerably. The path he'd taken was dark and shadowed, and the only sign of civilization she saw was the one unoccupied cabin they'd passed. Tall, snow-encrusted pines loomed over them, adding to the eeriness. Closing her eyes, Brooke rested her head against Marc's shoulders and waited for them to arrive at the cabin.

Unexpectedly, the snowmobile came to a slow, sputtering stop. Brooke lifted her head and frowned when she realized they were sitting out in the middle of nowhere, with the wind howling in the trees and cold chips of snow mingling with the flurries.

"Damn," Marc muttered, the one word as ominous as the elements surrounding them.

Brooke's heart leapt in her chest. "What's wrong?"

"I think we're out of gas." His tone was grim.

"What?" Unable to believe that could be true, she flipped up her face shield and peered over his shoulder at the illuminated panel between the handlebars. "The gauge says you still have a quarter of a tank."

"I know." He opened the gas cap on the metal tank in front of him and rocked the snowmobile with his thighs. They both listened intently for the slosh of liquid, and heard nothing. "The gauge must be stuck or broken, because we're completely empty." Unzipping his jacket, he pulled out his cell phone, pressed the on button, but didn't look hopeful as he stared at the digital display. "I can't call for help. We're out of range."

"Great," she said, dismounting the machinery and yanking off her helmet as adrenaline flowed through her. Fear, dread, and the accumulation of frustration from that evening's events mingled into a potent combination, and she jabbed an accusing finger his way. "Just great, Jamison! Here we are stranded somewhere off the beaten path of God knows where, without anyone knowing where we are. Even on the off chance that Shane or someone else came looking for us they wouldn't find us because you didn't take the normal route!"

He removed his helmet and stabbed his fingers through his hair. "Stop yelling," he said, his voice even and composed.

"Like it matters!" she shouted even louder, and threw up her arms to emphasize her point. "It's not as though there is anyone around to hear me."

"I hear you just fine, and you're making it difficult for me to think."

"If you were *thinking*, we wouldn't be in this predicament in the first place." She paced in front of the snowmobile, dismayed to realize that with each step she was sinking up to her calves in the fresh layer of snow. Not a good sign.

Trying to keep a clear head and her perspective on the situation, she glanced ahead, where the beam from the headlight barely penetrated the sheet of white in front of them. "How much further ahead do you think our cabin is?"

Hooking his helmet on the handlebar, he swung a long leg over the seat and stepped off the snowmobile. Very carefully, and without meeting her gaze, he said, "I'm not sure."

Brooke's stomach dropped to her knees and she gaped at him. "What do you mean, you're not sure?

You said you knew a short cut. We should have been to the cabin by now, or at least be close enough to walk there in a few minutes."

"I agree, but I think I veered off too far to the right at that cutoff a ways back." He braced his fists on his hips and worked his mouth in thought. "I don't remember seeing that cabin we passed when I took this short cut yesterday."

"You mean you don't know where we are?"

"I know *approximately* where we are."

"Approximately?" Her voice rose to a hysterical pitch when she realized the ramifications of his statement. "We have a major storm heading in and you're not even sure where we are or what direction it is to our cabin?"

He cast her a placating look. "Brooke, calm down."

Furious at him for numerous reasons, most of which stemmed from her lousy evening at the lodge, she bent down and scooped up a gloveful of snow and packed it into a solid ball. Then she vented. "Don't...tell...me...*what to do!*" She pitched the snowball at him and gained a measure of satisfaction when it splattered on his chest.

An annoyed frown creased his brows. "Dammit, Brooke, stop it."

Rebelliously, she immediately formed another one and threw it, and he ducked as her icy bullet came precariously close to his head. She continued her assault on Marc, heedless of the frigid air and the large, moist clumps of snow eddying around them. He cursed and held his arms up to ward off her blows, but she managed a few good shots.

She ranted and raved, and irrational or not considering the circumstances, the release felt so, so good. She'd learned from an early age to keep her feelings bottled up inside, not wanting to burden anyone else with her emotions when she was supposed to be the strong one. Now, the irritation she'd experienced at the lodge took precedence, making Marc an easy target.

He tried to reason with her, but she was too intent on making him suffer. She cursed him and his short cut that had stranded them. She insulted his lousy sense of direction. She addressed every issue but the one that really had her riled.

And then the rogue started laughing, which increased her temper. As she dipped down to scoop up more ammunition, he unexpectedly lunged toward her. Eyes wide in surprise, she tried to escape him, but her boots felt heavy, her legs like rubber. She turned, only to have him snag her around the waist and tackle her. She twisted in his embrace and cried out as she fell, burying her backside a foot deep in snow. Marc landed on top of her with a muffled "oomph." His ragged breath was blessedly warm on her face, and his large body sheltered her from the wind and falling snow. The weight of his body, however, threatened her sanity and caused a liquid rush of desire to spread through her veins.

Before she could react, his mouth came down on hers, hard, demanding and incredibly possessive. She gasped as the shocking contrast of his cold lips gave way to the delicious heat of his mouth, then the incendiary stroke of his tongue against hers. He kissed her deeply, aggressively, possibly punishing her for her numerous hits with those snowballs.

Reminding herself that she was mad at him, she

jerked her lips from his and pushed at his shoulders. She struggled beneath him, but he wouldn't budge. In frustration, she blurted out, "I bet you're sorry you didn't leave with that blonde, aren't you?" As soon as the words left her mouth, she instantly regretted the outburst.

It was dark outside, darker still cocooned beneath him, but she saw the corner of his mouth hitch up in a cocky grin. "Ahh, now we're getting to the crux of your attitude."

She set her jaw and said nothing. She'd revealed too much already.

"You're jealous," he murmured, his tone oddly affectionate.

"I am *not*," she refuted adamantly, unable to admit the truth to him. It was difficult enough admitting the truth to herself! "Being jealous would imply that I care about your sex life and who you date."

"And you don't care?" he asked, amusement threading his rich, husky voice.

"No," she replied primly.

"Liar." His expression softened, and a gust of air left his lungs, rife with resignation. "Just for the record, that other woman at the lodge was just a diversion from all those sexy signals you were sending off earlier. But it didn't work. I still don't want any woman but *you*."

With that startling revelation, he pushed off her and stood, then offered her his gloved hand. "Come on, we need to find shelter."

Knowing now was not the time to pursue his comment, she accepted his assistance. Ducking her head against an onslaught of flurries, she followed him back to the snowmobile, where he opened the compartment under the seat and withdrew a flashlight and a small emergency survival kit containing flares, matches, dried food and other necessities.

Now that the heat of her anger had been purged, the severity of their situation hit Brooke full force. Her teeth began to chatter and a chill slithered down her spine. She reached for her insulated helmet and slipped it over her head, knowing she'd need the added warmth. "If you're not sure where we are, or what direction the cabin is in, what are we going to do?"

He switched on the flashlight then turned off the snowmobile's headlamp. Pocketing the keys, he swung the small replacement beam back toward the way they'd come. "Our choices are limited. Staying here isn't an option, so we're going to have to head back to that cabin we saw and stay there for the night, or until this storm passes."

5

"THERE'S THE CABIN, just up ahead," Marc said to Brooke as his flashlight beam finally lit on a small structure coated in snow, a welcome sight that would provide them with the warmth and shelter they desperately needed. His thighs burned with the effort of trudging through knee-deep snow and leaning against the fierce gusts. He imagined Brooke was experiencing the same agony, but she hadn't issued any complaints.

"Thank God," came her muffled response through the shield of her helmet as she plodded along next to him. "I was beginning to think you'd misjudged your sense of direction again."

Though her tone held a wry note, she clearly sounded relieved, as was he. What had taken minutes by snowmobile had taken nearly an hour by foot. The winds, icy snow, and poor visibility had worked against them, and though he'd never admit it to Brooke, Marc *had* started to worry that he'd gotten them completely lost.

The emergency survival kit was tucked securely in his jacket, but the last thing he wanted was to test its reliability against the fury of a blizzard. Despite the fact that they were protected from head to toe in insulated gear and that the walking had kept their blood heated and flowing, the freezing temperature had managed to creep through seams and small openings, sending an occasional shiver coursing through him.

Once they were under the awning of the tiny porch and deemed the place deserted, Marc looked around for the best way to break into the cabin. Knowing he had little choice, he busted open one of the four small panes of glass that made up the front window, then reached inside with a gloved hand and unlatched the lock. He shoved up the wooden casing, and brushed away the sharp remnants of glass.

"You'll fit through that space better than I will," he said, motioning Brooke over.

She nodded in agreement, and seconds later she'd slipped safely inside the cabin and had the front door open for him to enter. He shoved the door closed behind him, and they both removed their helmets and looked around.

It wasn't much warmer in the cabin, but at least they had a roof over their heads and amenities for the duration of the storm. The structure wasn't anything fancy, definitely a vacation retreat. One sweeping glance of his flashlight encompassed a carpeted living room with a single couch in front of the fireplace, a kitchen with a small table, a bathroom off to the left, and an upstairs loft.

Marc hit one of the switches on the wall, and they both grinned as the lamp on the end table illuminated the room, indicating that the owners kept the electricity supply on. Heading into the kitchen, he turned on the sink's faucet, and wasn't surprised to discover the water had been turned off so the pipes wouldn't freeze. They checked the cupboards and found them stocked with bottled water, canned and packaged foods, and airtight containers holding other staples.

"See what you can find to cover up that hole in the front window," he said, heading back through the adjoining living room to the front door. "I'm going back outside to see if I can locate the valves to turn on the water."

Within an hour, the place was as intimate and cozy as their own cabin. They had running water, along with gas for the water heater and stove. While Marc had been scouring the perimeter of the cabin for those valves, he'd discovered a crate of wood. Against the fierce elements, he'd hauled every last log into the house, and Brooke had patched the window with a piece of cardboard and nails she'd discovered in the back utility room. Though they could hear the wind whistling through cracks and still feel an occasional draft, it was nothing compared to spending the night outside in the company of the storm.

After stripping off his snowsuit and gloves, Marc joined Brooke by the fire. Rubbing his chilled hands together, he glanced at her, immediately picking up on the worry lining her features.

The urge to touch her was strong, and with effort he restrained the tender impulse. He'd revealed way too much after that kiss in the snow, more than he'd intended. If she hadn't known before, she certainly realized now that she had him confused and frustrated, and completely tied up in knots, despite his attempt to divert their attraction by fraternizing with another woman. The only thing his efforts had accomplished was to make him more aware of Brooke.

Maintaining distance during their seclusion and not

taking advantage of their attraction was going to zap every bit of restraint and control he possessed. She knew as well as he did that nothing could come of them being together, no matter how much they both wanted one another. Above all, he treasured his friendship with Brooke, and the possibility of heartache and other emotional complications was too high to risk. They'd already skirted that particular danger with the seductive kisses they'd indulged in, and he knew making love would only up the ante to a level he wasn't prepared to invest in.

And since he wasn't the kind of guy to carry an emergency condom in his wallet, keeping his hands off her was a matter of principle as well as practicality. Never mind that there were a dozen other ways he imagined making love to her that didn't require a prophylactic.

He watched her chew on her full lower lip and ignored the deep clenching of desire in his belly. "Hey, you okay?"

She inhaled a deep breath, momentarily drawing his gaze to the way her breasts rose and fell beneath her tightly knit sweater. "Jessica is probably frantic right about now," she said, turning her deep blue gaze his way. "I really wish there was some way we could reach her and let her know we're both okay. It would make the next day or so easier to get through knowing she wasn't worrying about us. There's a CB radio back in our cabin that Jessica knows about for emergencies. I'm sure she's turned it on by now since we haven't returned, but I guess that does *us* little good."

He grasped a way to ease Brooke's concern. "Unless I can call out on my cell phone." He hated to offer false hope, but he couldn't discount the chance that he might be able to transmit from this area.

Heading back to his snowsuit by the door, he retrieved the unit from his jacket and turned it on. The signal remained non-existent. Not willing to overlook any realm of possibility, he meticulously strolled around the cabin, covering every inch of space...and finally found a two-foot area near the front window that afforded him a signal, albeit a weak one.

"Got it," he said, grinning victoriously at Brooke, who returned the smile. He dialed 911, and after he explained their predicament, the dispatcher forwarded his call to the ranger's station for help.

Five minutes later, he disconnected the line and headed back toward Brooke, who was kneeling in front of the fireplace and tossing more logs onto the grate. "Now that the ranger station has your CB channel, they'll keep trying to call our cabin until they get hold of someone and assure them that we're safe and okay."

"Good." After arranging the wood with the poker, she stood and set the screen back in place then brushed off her hands. "What about us?"

He placed his phone on the coffee table, next to a small pile of magazines. "They know our location—"

"*Approximately*," she cut in, her voice infused with a teasing note.

"Yeah, approximately," he reluctantly agreed. Like any other male, he was loathe to admit that he wasn't exactly certain of their whereabouts. "The guy I spoke with said that as long as we aren't in an emergency situation we need to stay put until the white-out conditions improve and they can send out their rescue team."

"And when did they think that would be?"

"According to the National Weather Service, there's another storm right behind this current one. They're expecting four to six feet of snow in the next day or two, without much relief in between."

The implications of his statement couldn't be more obvious. Instead of the apprehension or reservation he would have expected from Brooke, his sister-in-law, an alluring smile curved the mouth of Brooke, the newly confident woman. "Then it's just you and me alone until the blizzard passes."

Marc's heart thumped hard in his chest. The sudden sexy gleam in Brooke's gaze didn't bode well for him, his libido, or his willpower.

THEIR SITUATION WAS RIPE with opportunity, and teeming with endless possibilities. Marc, however, wasn't cooperating with Brooke's plan for seduction. Ever since calling the ranger station and imparting the news of their two-day confinement, he'd opted for light and amicable conversation, and avoided close proximity.

That arrangement would change, and soon, considering they'd be sharing the makeshift bed they'd made in front of the fireplace. Neither one of them felt comfortable sleeping in someone else's bed, so they'd opted to spread open a large, flannel-lined sleeping bag they'd found in the closet, and use the pillows and blankets from the loft. The bed was soft, comfortable, and afforded them both their own separate space—*if* they wanted it.

Marc apparently did, considering how neatly he'd

aligned his own blanket and two pillows on *his* side of the sleeping bag.

Luckily, she had two days to sway and convince him, to wear down his resistance and lead them both astray.

Releasing a deep sigh to waylay the desire curling low in her belly, she glanced toward the gorgeous, tempting man in the kitchen who'd insisted on making them each a mug of prepackaged hot chocolate before they turned in for the night. She wasn't the least bit tired. Now that her adrenaline surge from their hike through the storm had dissipated, and her initial worry about the others back at their cabin had been eased, her thoughts were focused on the various ways she might entice Marc into accepting her proposition.

Unfortunately, he was being way too chivalrous, and though the old Brooke would have appreciated his gallant attempt to resist her, the newly blossoming Brooke had decided to have this affair and enjoy every aspect of it. Stranded in this little cabin, she didn't have a care in the world, just a burning desire to explore the depths of her sensuality and passion with Marc...no promises involved.

The arrangement should suit Marc perfectly, just as soon as she broke through his reserve.

Figuring tonight was a bust considering everything they'd been through, she sat up and peeled her sweater over her head and tossed it onto the couch, then shimmied out of her leggings, leaving her clad in her long-sleeved thermal top and bottoms etched with tiny pink hearts—nothing remotely sexy or appealing about that! Then she wrangled her way out of her confining bra through her top, and added that to the pile. Removing the elastic band at the base of the French braid she'd worn, she unraveled the strands and massaged her tight scalp. When she turned around, she gasped to find Marc standing by the sofa, two mugs of steaming cocoa in his hands and a lopsided grin on his face that belied the dark, smoldering gray of his irises.

His gaze took in her form-fitting underwear. "I think I have a new appreciation for thermals," he murmured.

This was the flirtatious Marc she knew and felt comfortable with. The inherently sexual man who'd accommodate her request when the time came. "Uh-huh," she said, rolling her eyes at his claim, no matter how complimentary. "I find it hard to believe any man would find thermal appealing. It ranks right up there with flannel."

Marc chuckled, the rich sound filled with relaxed amusement. "It's what's underneath all that thermal that counts. Peeling away all those soft, warm layers to reveal even warmer, softer skin could prove to be a very exciting experience."

Oh, yeah, she thought, knowing she wouldn't object if he decided to do just that with her.

He reached out...and handed her one of the mugs of hot chocolate. "This ought to warm your belly before you fall asleep."

She accepted his offering and grinned when she saw the smooth white blob floating on top of her drink. "Hey, where did you find marshmallows?"

"It's marshmallow cream, the kind that comes in a jar." He placed his mug on the coffee table in front of their makeshift bed. "It was in the cupboard."

Settling back down on her side of the sleeping bag,

she crossed her legs facing the hearth and waited for Marc to join her.

The lamp behind her snapped off, but the bright fire provided more than enough illumination to make up for the loss of light. She glanced at her watch—it was ten after eleven and definitely bedtime. After the day they'd had she should have been ready to crash, yet she decided if Marc was going to be noble and not touch her, then she wouldn't mind just talking for a while.

Wrapping her fingers around her mug, she brought it to her lips and took a sip. She savored the luxuriant flavor of chocolate filling her mouth, then licked off a smudge of marshmallow that clung to her upper lip. Behind her, she heard the arousing rustle of Marc removing his sweater, the heart-pounding sound of his jeans' zipper, and the scrape of that rough material dragging down his legs before he stepped out of it.

When he joined her in front of the fire, his attire matched hers, minus the pink hearts. She couldn't resist teasing him. "You don't look half-bad in thermal, either." On the contrary, the nubby fabric molded to every hard contour of his body. Judging by the lack of bumps or lines around his hips and thighs, he wasn't wearing any briefs.

He retrieved his hot chocolate off the coffee table, and he flashed a sexy grin.

She watched as he stretched out on his side and propped himself up with his elbow. Taking another drink of the warm liquid, she decided on more stimulating conversation. "I'll bet Stacey and Shane wish they were the ones who were stranded in this storm, instead of us."

He slanted her a curious glance over the rim of his mug. "How so?"

She grinned. "They'd definitely make the most of the seclusion."

He said nothing, though she knew Marc had followed the implication behind her statement—why weren't *they* taking advantage of the isolation that had so conveniently presented itself?

Since he wasn't cooperating with her discussion, she continued. "I have to admit that I've always been a little envious of Stacey, and how she can just enjoy having an affair with a man she's attracted to, no strings attached."

He considered that for a moment. "And you wish you could be like that?"

"In some ways." She shrugged, and set her empty mug on the coffee table. "I've only recently given it any thought, but it doesn't seem as easy for a woman to just have a physical relationship with a man without gaining a certain kind of reputation."

A smile tipped up the corner of his mouth. "Ahh, the old double standard."

"Yes. It's unfair how it seems acceptable for a man to play the field, but when a woman does the same thing she risks her virtue or respectability."

He mulled over her comment while staring into the depths of his mug, then glanced her way. "Are we talking about the double standard within the bonds of marriage, or being single and unattached?"

"Both, actually." She drew her slender legs up and wrapped her arms around her knees. "I know society has come a long way and we're living in the twenty-first century, but it just seems easier and more acceptable for men to go out and have a fling than for a woman to do the same thing."

"I don't believe in double standards when it comes to sex and relationships," he replied. "A good sexual chemistry should be enjoyed by both partners, for as long as the attraction lasts."

"No commitments, huh?" she asked softly.

He met her stare evenly. "No commitments, Brooke," he said, the statement sounding too much like a warning. "I *avoid* serious relationships."

She rested her chin atop her knees, a compelling blend of curiosity and tenderness weaving through her. "Why?"

He scrubbed a hand over his stubbled jaw, his frown giving her the distinct impression that he'd rather ignore her question. She waited patiently for his reply, wanting to know the reasons why he'd chosen the bachelor route and was so against something permanent with a woman.

As if realizing she wasn't going to let the subject slide, he finally answered. "I learned early on that I don't have what it takes to sustain a lasting commitment." A muscle in his cheek ticked with irritation. "The women I've dated know my rules right up front. I don't make promises I can't keep."

Brooke knew there was more to Marc's statement than a cavalier attitude about relationships. There was something deeper and infinitely emotional behind his words—the misery creasing his expression told a tale of its own. Whatever he'd been through had affected his ability to believe he could be the kind of man a woman wanted for a husband.

"What I see is what I get, huh?" She tossed his own

words back at him, suddenly seeing them as an emotional shield he hid behind when things got too intense. Didn't he realize that he'd given her too many glimpses past the surface of that carefree, flirtatious demeanor for her to think him so shallow? She'd seen a side to Marc she hadn't known existed until this weekend, a man with integrity whom she trusted, a man very different from the one he believed himself to be, or the one he presented to everyone else.

"That just about sums it up, Brooke." Abruptly, he stood and picked up her mug from the coffee table. "It's late, it's been a long, exhausting day, and I think we both need to get some rest."

He stalked off toward the kitchen, and Brooke let him go, seeing his exit for the diversion it was. She'd touched on personal issues and struck a nerve somewhere. She'd also broached the subject of an affair in a subtle, but unmistakable way. In return, he'd set down his unbendable rules with her, letting her know under no circumstances did he waver from his convictions.

She was forewarned, but not discouraged in the least. She understood and accepted his rules, and she still wanted him and the culmination of pleasure that his kisses evoked.

But for tonight, she'd give him a reprieve. They were both exhausted, and she wanted to be at her freshest when she seduced him. Tomorrow was another day of seclusion, and she wouldn't be as easily denied.

BROOKE GRADUALLY WOKE to the smell of freshly brewed coffee, and the sexy sight of Marc standing in the kitchen by the sink, holding a mug in his hand while he stared out the window. There wasn't much to see outside except a swirl of white, which confirmed they were in the throes of the furious storm sweeping through the Rocky Mountains.

Seemingly deep in thought, he sighed heavily and shifted his stance. The muscles bisecting his back rippled with the movement beneath his thermal shirt, and his jean-clad hip rocked to the side. A small smile played around her mouth as she enjoyed the masculine view—until he turned around and glanced her way, meeting her sleepy gaze. His ebony hair was damp, and the dark stubble lining his jaw and cheeks made his eyes appear black and intense.

A feathery sensation coursed through her, prompting instantaneous awareness. Indeed, the erotic fantasies that had invaded her dreams last night had deepened her aching need for him.

"Morning," she murmured, her voice husky with the remnants of sleep.

"Morning," he returned, then took a drink of the steaming brew in his mug. "How are you feeling?"

Tossing off her covers, she stood, then groaned as muscles she didn't even know she possessed screamed in protest. "Oh, man," she breathed in agony.

The corner of his mouth quirked with amusement. "I think you just answered my question. I woke up in the same sorry condition."

She smiled. "I feel like every tendon from my neck to calves is going to snap if I straighten too fast." Slowly, she reached her arms over her head and arched her back, and winced as her body reluctantly distended. The exercise caused her breasts to thrust forward and her top to lift, exposing a two-inch strip of flesh. He noticed, his gaze lingering, searing her skin.

An annoyed frown creased his brow and he averted his gaze, placing his mug on the counter. "A hot shower will help relax your muscles."

"Sounds wonderful," she agreed, gratified to see that despite his lecture and good intentions last night he was struggling with his own desire. Heading into the kitchen area, she glanced at her watch. It was twenty after eight. "Have you been up long?"

"For a while," he said vaguely, giving her the impression that he'd had a restless night. "I called the ranger station this morning. They confirmed that they got a hold of Shane late last night and gave him the message that we were fine and safe."

"I'm glad." Knowing that Jessica wouldn't spend the next day or so panicking over their whereabouts was a big relief. "Any change in the weather?" she asked, dragging a hand through her disheveled hair.

His jaw tightened. "No." He didn't sound happy about that fact. Turning away from her, he retrieved a frying pan from below the gas stove and set it on a burner. "Why don't you go take a shower while I make us some breakfast? I found some shampoo, soap, toothpaste and mouthwash, and I left it out for you to use."

"Thanks." Heading into the bathroom, she turned on the water, stripped off her clothes, and stepped beneath the shower spray.

Her head fell forward, and a groan of relief purred in her throat as the hot, pulsating water pounded across her stiff shoulders, loosening muscles and gradually relaxing her body. She shampooed her hair, then soaped up a face cloth and washed from neck to ankle. She turned around to rinse, and gasped as the hard stream of water pelted her sensitive breasts, causing her nipples to peak, then flowed down her belly and trickled between her thighs like the tantalizing stroke of liquid silk.

She shuddered as a shameless kind of pleasure beckoned, swirling around her as feverishly as the steam from the hot water. Closing her eyes, she cupped her hands over her heavy breasts and kneaded the firm flesh, brushed her fingers over the taut crests. Her breathing grew shallow, and her heart pounded hard in her chest.

The need Marc had ignited with his sexy kisses was just as vibrant, just as demanding. Biting her lower lip, she slowly slicked her palms down her stomach, let her fingers graze the thatch of soft curls at the apex of her thighs. Her belly tightened, and her thighs trembled in expectation of that first touch, a deeper caress, and the incredible, shuddering release that would follow.

It would be so easy to take the edge off the desire thrumming through her. Instead, she stopped before indulging in the intimate touch that would end her torment, opting to let the ache and anticipation build.

Marc had roused that sensual hunger within her. *He* would be the one to appease it.

6

"I MADE A PIG of myself." Brooke set her fork on her empty plate and pushed it aside. "I've never eaten six pancakes in one sitting before."

Seated across from Brooke at the small table in the kitchen, Marc chuckled as she pressed a hand to her full stomach, her expression dismayed. "I guess you were hungrier than you'd realized." There certainly hadn't been anything spectacular about the pancakes he'd made from the mix he'd found in the cupboard, or the butter flavored syrup they'd poured on top.

"Hmm," she replied, the sound rumbling sensually in her throat. A slow smile graced her lips, and her gaze took on a shimmering quality that tempted and teased. Hunger took on another meaning altogether.

The insinuation behind that vague response and her body language wasn't lost on Marc. Ever since she'd returned from her shower, she'd been openly flirting with him, heightening the awareness between them.

The woman had seduction on her mind, and he feared his sanity and libido wouldn't survive the length of the storm. Obviously, openly admitting to a love-'em-and-leave-'em attitude hadn't deterred her campaign to tempt him, as he'd hoped.

She stood and leaned across the table, reaching for his plate, unerringly drawing his gaze to her breasts, which swayed forward with the movement and pressed full and round against her top. The chafe of fabric caused her nipples to peak and his groin to stir. She hadn't put her bra back on after her shower, and wore only her leggings and thermal shirt. The cabin was warm enough that they didn't need more than that.

She stacked his dish and utensils on top of hers. "Since you made breakfast, I suppose the least I can do is clean up the mess."

He swallowed the offer to help along with the last of his coffee, knowing it was best if they kept their distance. The entire day stretched ahead of them, impossibly long and filled with too many appealing scenarios he was determined to avoid.

"Great." He abruptly stood. "I'll go start another fire."

Kneeling before the brick hearth, he removed the screen. He stacked pieces of wood on the grate, stuffed pieces of crumpled paper beneath the logs, and struck a match to ignite the flame. Despite his resolve to resist Brooke, that didn't stop his gaze from continually drifting her way as she cleared the table and washed dirty dishes.

Though she'd towel-dried her hair and combed the strands away from her face, the ends were still damp from her shower. Her skin had been scrubbed clean of makeup, and she looked natural and wholesome, and more beautiful than any of the sophisticated, cosmetically enhanced women he'd dated over the years. She attracted him on too many levels, but it was the way she tugged on his emotional wants and needs that completely disarmed him.

He shook off the sentiment and focused on stoking the fire. Too soon, she joined him, sitting on the sleeping bag a few feet away from him. Neither one of them had folded their blankets or made their beds—why bother when they'd be there at least another night?

She reached for one of the women's magazines on the coffee table and absently thumbed through the glossy pages. After a moment of skimming the contents, she said, "Now here's an interesting quiz. 'Take our sizzling sex survey and tell us about your sex life.' What do you say you and I fill in the blanks and see how we measure up?"

After placing the poker on the brass rack, Marc straightened the screen in front of the blazing fire, then sat across from her, unable to miss the daring light in her eyes. He turned the magazine his way and perused the article. "You sure about that? Some of these questions are really personal."

"I'm game if you are." She grinned impudently. "It'll pass time, which we have plenty of, and our answers could prove to be quite entertaining."

And enlightening, he thought, and knew that was the purpose of her challenge. Knowing she was intent on seducing him regardless of his efforts to resist her, he decided to play into her scheme. He'd be aggressive and push her as far as he could, until she realized she was engaging in a risky game with irreversible, emotional repercussions. Hopefully, she'd rethink her plan to tempt and tease him before she made a big mistake she would regret later.

And most important, this way he'd maintain control of the situation right from the start.

"All right, I'll take the survey with you. And there'll be no cheating or fibbing," he said.

She wrinkled her nose at him and affected an amusing, prim attitude. "I don't cheat or fib."

"That's good to hear." He stretched out on his side, propped his head in his palm, and patted the sleeping bag in front of him. "And you need to come down here so I can look you in the eyes while we're answering our questions."

She hesitated for a brief moment. He supposed she felt a semblance of security sitting upright, elevated above him, but he wasn't going to allow any distance between them. If she planned to push boundaries, he was going to push right back.

She scooted low, until she lay on her side facing him. They weren't touching physically, but a keen sense of intimacy surrounded them.

"Better?" she asked.

Smiling his approval, he nodded. "Much. Let's get started." Pushing the sleeves of his thermal shirt up to his forearms, he glanced at the magazine open between them. "When was your last sexual encounter? Yesterday, last week, one to six months ago, six to nine months ago, or over a year?"

He lifted his gaze, meeting Brooke's expectantly, and her stomach took a steep, unexpected dive. Embarrassed to admit just how long it had been since she'd been with a man, she said, "You go first."

He squinted up at the low-beamed ceiling and thought for a moment. "My last sexual encounter would fall in the category of six to nine months ago."

Without a doubt, his reply shocked Brooke—the man was so earthy and physical she'd always imagined he indulged freely in sex. She liked that he was discriminating when it came to whom he slept with. She also realized he hadn't been with a woman since before their first kiss three months ago.

His candid response eased the way for hers. "Mine was over a year ago."

His gaze glittered with too much heat. "Abstinence and the anticipation of wanting someone makes for some of the best sex."

A delicious shiver lapped at her nerve endings, the compelling sensation spreading through her like warm molasses. "I suppose it does," she said breathlessly.

Grinning as if he was enjoying himself, he bent his head back over the test, causing a thick shock of black hair to fall over his forehead. With the light from the fire casting shadows over his face he looked like a sexy renegade.

His body tensed as he perused the next question, and his flirtatious smile faded. "Have you ever engaged in a one-night stand?"

"No." Her reply was immediate. "Have you?"

Slowly, he lifted his head. "Yeah," he admitted with obvious reluctance. "Once. Years ago."

The guilt and regret etching his lean features concerned and bewildered her. "Was the incident that bad?"

He hesitated, scrubbing a hand over the stubble lining his clenched jaw. "It was the circumstances surrounding the one-night stand. It never should have happened."

Whatever had occurred, whatever the reasons, the encounter had affected him deeply. Curiosity stirred within her, as well as the knowledge that despite his

carefree bachelor appearance, Marc didn't possess the
cavalier attitude toward women and sex that she'd
thought he did...that his *brother* did. The revelation
was stunning, and reassuring in a way she didn't want
to contemplate.

Curving her arm around her pillow, she tucked it
more fully beneath her head. "Next question?" she
prompted brightly, anxious to change the subject for
his sake.

He looked grateful for her move to dispel the too-
serious mood that had settled between them. "Hmm,"
he said, considering the next topic up for deliberation.
"If you weren't in a relationship, would you be willing
to have a hot, wild fling with someone who completely
turned you on?"

Brooke's skin tightened and tingled at the underlying insinuation in that simple survey question. The
statement addressed an issue they'd been avoiding
since yesterday morning's kiss and challenged her new
dictum to *just do it*. It also tested that wall of resistance
Marc had erected between them.

He hesitated, seemingly struggling with his answer.
Finally his long, sooty lashes swept upward, revealing
eyes that had darkened to charcoal. "As much as I wish
I could say no, I'd be lying. I've considered it."

With you. The unspoken words hung in the air.
Brooke's pulse raced, and her lips parted on a rush of
breath. A foot of distance separated them, but that
made little difference in her body's reaction to those
sultry bedroom eyes, the rich, warm tone of his voice.
His deliberate words. Her breasts swelled, and she
grew moist between her thighs, which she pressed
tightly together. His direct, masculine stare definitely

turned her on, seducing her mind, making her ache to feel those callused hands of his skimming her naked skin, to feel his lips and tongue exploring *everywhere.*

A moan slipped past her throat at the provocative image filling her head. Mortified that she'd gotten so carried away, she reined in her lustful fantasy.

His smile turned sinfully confident, too knowing. "I take it you agree?" he asked huskily.

She nodded mutely, not trusting herself to speak. Especially when she realized how aroused he'd become just by watching her face, her expression, and hearing the frustrated sound she'd made. His erection jutted against the front of his pants, full and long and incredibly thick.

Without a hint of embarrassment, he angled his leg toward her on the sleeping bag to adjust his position to a more comfortable one. "Shall we go on?" he asked nonchalantly.

A subtle dare, though he was giving her the opportunity to call a halt to this crazy game. Electrifying heat poured over her and shimmered between them, prompting her to explore the depths and boundaries of the sensuality Marc was awakening.

"Go ahead," she whispered.

Lowering his gaze, he skimmed his index finger down the numbered sentences on the page. Dark brows raised with interest as he read, "Would you be open to experiencing new and different sexual positions and techniques that your partner might suggest?"

That sexy grin of his made another appearance. "Sure. Variety is a good thing. It keeps a couple's sex life fun and exciting."

"I'll take your word for it," she said, then grimaced when she realized exactly what she'd revealed—that her sex life hadn't included much variety. There hadn't been much fun or excitement, either. Eric had been just as serious in the bedroom as he'd been outside of it.

Marc splayed his big hand on the opposite side of the survey page, his long, tapered fingers reaching the edges. "You didn't answer the question," he said, not allowing her to retreat on any level. "Yes or no to shedding inhibitions?"

He couldn't have known about her vow to explore her sexuality, yet his eyes glimmered with a hot, intense perception. She swallowed hard and replied, "Yes, I'd do it."

The corner of his mouth curved with lazy humor, and he continued on. "Have you ever brought yourself to orgasm?"

Brooke's pulse thudded, and she pressed her palms to her burning cheeks. "You can't be serious!"

A warm, deep chuckle filled the cozy space between them. "I wouldn't make up something like that. It's right here, see?"

She leaned close, verifying his claim. Her face flamed brighter.

"I'll go first," he offered, his breath warm against her cheek since she hadn't moved back.

She lifted her head and rolled her eyes. "Considering most boys discover at an early age how good *that* feels, I already know *your* answer."

"I think this magazine is referring to a *man* gratifying himself." He worked his mouth back and forth in thought. "Why don't we rephrase the question? How about...have you brought yourself to orgasm within the past six months?"

She gaped at him. "Can we just *skip* this question?"

"No, now you've got me curious—unless you'd rather stop the survey altogether?"

She got the distinct impression that he was hoping for just that, but she wasn't willing to call it quits. "No, go ahead."

Amusement gleamed in his eyes. "Well, since it's been almost nine months since I've been with a woman, and we are being *honest*, I'd have to say yes, I've brought myself to orgasm in the past six months."

An erotic mental image popped into Brooke's mind before she could stop it, of Marc magnificently naked and aroused, on the verge of ecstasy as his fist stroked his erection in a tight, wet rhythm...

"I guess that blush on your face speaks for itself, huh?"

If he only knew! Her arm clenched the pillow tighter, and she cursed the heaviness between her thighs. She shifted her legs, and nearly gasped at the exquisite friction against her swollen, inflamed flesh. "Yes," she said, her voice raspy.

"Yes, what?"

The man had no shame! "Yes, I've resorted to self-gratification in the past six months," she said between gritted teeth.

His breath left his chest in an audible whoosh. He blinked heavily, scrutinizing her with eyes gradually glazing over with lust. Suspecting that he was entertaining his own personal fantasy, starring *her* in the same role she'd just imagined *him*, she tapped the magazine to redirect his attention. "Next question, Marc."

He shook himself back to the present, then searched to find where they'd left off. "What is your favorite sexual position?" He rubbed his thumb along his chin before answering. "Whatever feels good at the time."

She drew a deep breath that did little to help her regain her composure. "I like being on top."

"Oh, yeah," he agreed, his devastating grin matching his dark good looks. "That feels good *anytime*."

His eyes went downcast again as he consulted the survey. "Have you ever had multiple orgasms with one partner in a single night?" His chest puffed out a fraction. "Yeah, though I do need time to recuperate in between."

She stifled a grin at his typical male pride, even while she appreciated that he was a generous, giving lover. "I'm impressed."

He lifted a dark brow, silently turning the tables on her. *Have you ever had multiple orgasms?*

At the moment, she was so aroused she felt as though she could have a dozen in rapid succession. She shook her head. "No."

He glanced down at the page, then back up again. "Would you like to?"

Her stomach pitched sideways and a flood of liquid desire weakened her limbs. She eyed him warily, wondering if the man could read minds. "Is *that* on the survey?"

His gaze searched her face, too intently. "No, personal curiosity."

She bit her bottom lip as a slow swell of excitement pounded through her at the thought of indulging in such luxurious, all-consuming pleasure...of freeing her body of all mental restrictions and wallowing in wave after wave of the purest ecstasy a woman could experience. To be greedy, and revel in a man worshiping her body with his mouth and hands, caressing her in carnal ways, discovering sensitive regions and plying her with sensual delights beyond her comprehension.

Brooke tugged at the collar of her thermal top, suddenly burning up. She felt hot and achy and needy...and wondered if she'd have to go outside and roll in the snow to cool off. The icy bath might help the fever spreading across her skin; unfortunately, it wouldn't do much to soothe the fretful knot pulling tighter and tighter inside her. She couldn't remember ever feeling so hot and bothered. So sexually aware of her body.

He waited patiently, *shamelessly*, for her answer.

She cleared her throat. "I don't think it's that easy for a woman to achieve multiple orgasms." Her reply was deliberately evasive, a testimony of her own personal inexperience and an attempt to usher them on to the next phase of the quiz.

"Depends on the woman's partner." The rumbling, seductive undertone to his voice mesmerized her, as did his eyes. "Most women are incredibly sensitive after their first orgasm, but if they relax and you touch them just the right way, soft and slow and gradually build up to a steady rhythm again..."

Brooke's breathing grew ragged, and she held up a hand to halt his outrageous, stimulating monologue, certain she couldn't take much more without embarrassing herself. "I don't think this is relevant to the survey."

A satisfied smile played around the corners of his mouth. "Last question," he murmured, moving on, leaving her frustrated and her body throbbing with an excruciating need. "What arouses you the most?"

She groaned deep in her throat as a multitude of answers bombarded her. *Him. His words. His body. That promise of ultimate pleasure blazing in his eyes.*

He didn't mull over the question for long. "I get really turned on when I'm with a woman who isn't afraid to be aggressive and tell me what she wants or what feels good. How about you?"

Oh, she was feeling *very* aggressive. Shamelessly so. She was tempted to prove her assertiveness, to climb on top of him and kiss him senseless and let him do all those wicked, delicious things to her and anything else that entered that salacious mind of his. The reckless urge was so strong it took all her effort to restrain herself.

Emboldened with sexual confidence, she allowed a naughty smile to grace her lips. The man liked a woman who wasn't afraid to tell him what she wanted. This week, she was supposed to be that kind of brazen female. Tonight, she'd test her wiles.

Slowly, provocatively, she dampened her bottom lip with her tongue, and noticed that his eyes watched, and his body tensed. "What arouses me the most?" she repeated throatily, reveling in the power she possessed to excite him. "The way you kiss me," she whispered.

His nostrils flared at her admission, and his eyes flickered with something dark and predatory. As if she'd unleashed a sleeping tiger, he moved, quick and precise, a blur of tan cotton, fluid muscle and virile heat. In less than a heartbeat he had her pinned beneath his stunningly large body with his elbows trapping her arms at her sides, and a knee wedged between her thighs.

Their gazes locked, and their ragged breaths came in unison. They'd avoided touching one another all morning, instead arousing each other with words and mental images, which made this contact all the more electrifying. His unmistakable erection prodded her hip, throbbing with desire, matching the same pulse deep within her.

His callused fingers reached her mouth, stroked across the soft, sensitive flesh of her bottom lip. The smile that eased across his face was strangely tender, as if he coveted what he touched. "You're extremely easy to please," he murmured.

"I've never been kissed like that before," she admitted, baring herself and unearthing deeply buried secrets she hadn't intended to share with him. Despite all the sexy, personal things the survey had revealed, she suddenly felt very vulnerable and exposed. Somewhere along the way they'd gone from fun and playful, and crossed that forbidden line to something deeper and more serious.

An agonized groan rumbled up from his chest, and he buried his face in her neck, as if he, too, were struggling with some internal battle. His silky hair tickled her jaw, and his hot, moist breath caressed her throat. He shifted his weight, which caused his thigh to press against her sensitive core.

She inhaled sharply as sensations clamored within her. "Marc?" Her voice trembled with undeniable need.

The one word seemed to snap him out of his sensual haze. With a fierce curse, he rolled off her and moved away. Immediately, Brooke missed the warmth and intimacy of him lying on top of her.

He sat with his back braced against the couch and scrubbed both hands down his face, his features haggard with frustration. "I think our conversation has gotten *way* off track."

Brooke disagreed. They were finally *on track*, and she wasn't about to let this opportunity slip out of her reach.

She shifted to her knees, but didn't move closer. Not yet, anyway. "Remember that question on the survey?"

A startling combination of suspicion and sexual heat glowed in the depths of his gaze. "There were *many* questions on that survey," he said cautiously.

She touched her tongue to her upper lip, which had grown dry from a sudden bout of nerves. Seduction had never been her forte. "I'm talking about the one that asked if you'd be willing to have a hot, wild fling with someone who completely turned you on."

"Yeah, I remember," he said, his tone low and rough.

The thudding of her heart couldn't be calmed. "We both said yes."

His hands clenched into tight fists. "I said I've considered it."

"With me?" She needed to hear him say it.

He didn't disappoint her. "Yeah, with you."

A shudder passed through her, igniting her blood with anticipation. "Then we're even. I've considered it with you, too."

A harsh hiss of breath escaped him, and his big body

tensed. The very air around them seemed electrified, sizzling with energy and keen awareness.

"I think we've established that we turn each other on." A needy ache tightened her throat, her skin tingled, and her pulse quickened. "I want you, Marc. I want that hot, wild fling with *you*."

Shaking his head in denial, he pressed the heels of his palms against his eyes and gritted his teeth. "Brooke, I'm not sure this is a good idea." Doubts infused his gruff voice.

Feeling desperate, she crawled over to where he sat and knelt in front of him. Gently, she grabbed his wrists and pulled his hands away from his face, undeterred by his fierce expression. "I'm a big girl, Marc. We're both adults, and I'm going into this with my eyes wide-open, with no expectations other than fun and pleasure."

She looked at his big hands next to hers, his long fingers, and trembled at the thought of him touching her, caressing her. "I'm willing to take this as far as you're willing to go. No commitments, no promises and no regrets." She was offering him every bachelor's dream. Where most men would have leapt at her proposition, without conscience, thought or hesitation, Marc's internal struggle proved that he didn't take sex with her lightly.

"Brooke..." Her name on his lips sounded so sweet, so intimate, conflicting with the regret etching his lean features. Reaching out, he brushed her hair away from her cheek, then skimmed his knuckles gently along her jaw. "Not only is this not a smart idea, I don't have any protection with me."

Initial disappointment curled through her, and she

immediately squashed the emotion. She wasn't going to give him any excuses to deny her. "A minor technicality I'm sure we can work around. I'm willing to be as creative as our surroundings allow, and as innovative as you want to be."

His eyes darkened, and she imagined he was thinking of all the erotic ways they could pleasure one another. Still, he resisted, wavering between holding back, or accepting her sexy proposal.

She planned to push him over the edge, straight into bliss.

Moving closer, between his legs, she pressed her palms to his chest. Even through his shirt she could feel the heat and strength of him, and his wild heartbeat. Holding his gaze, she boldly slipped her hands down his torso, past the waistband of his jeans, and let her fingers trail lightly over the erection straining the fly of his pants.

He sucked in a swift breath, but didn't move, touch her, or try to remove her playful hand.

His willpower amazed her, and challenged her. Letting her lashes fall to half-mast, she smiled lazily, determined to shatter his control to obtain what she wanted. Recalling the words he'd used on her yesterday morning in the kitchen, she decided to turn the tables on him.

She leaned into him, until her mouth hovered near his ear and she cupped the proof of his desire for her more fully in her palm. "You're *definitely* curious," she murmured, then shivered as his hot, erratic breath stirred against her neck. "I'm tempted, we both want it, so let's do it and enjoy the time together."

He grasped her hand to stop her tantalizing caresses.

Lifting her head, she looked in his smoky-gray eyes, expecting a gentle rejection, not the ruthless glint she encountered.

"All right," he agreed, surprising her. "We'll have that hot, wild fling you want. But I want something in return." Bringing the hand that had stroked him to his lips, he placed a kiss in her palm and flicked his soft, warm tongue against the center.

She gasped, feeling that sensual lap all the way to the tips of her breasts. The sensation he evoked was delicious, and incredibly sinful. "What do you want in return?" she asked breathlessly.

"While we're here in this cabin, there is no saying no." He nibbled on the tip of one finger, then another, taking his sweet time toward her pinky. "No restrictions, no inhibitions. *Anything* goes."

Her belly tumbled at his frank request. His gaze was daring, and a trifle dangerous, but she refused to back down now that she'd come so far. Tilting her head, she injected a teasing note into her voice. "Aww, darn it, and here I left my padded handcuffs at home."

A dark brow arched wickedly. "Oh, I'm sure we can find a way to improvise on that fantasy, or any other you or I have in mind. Anything goes, Brooke," he reiterated, his gaze very direct and wholly male. "Agreed?"

She nodded. "Agreed."

He looked momentarily taken aback at her easy acquiescence. "You're willing to do anything I ask?"

She almost smiled at the surprise in his tone, and realized he'd fully expected her to refuse his outrageous terms. "*Anything*, Marc."

He released her hand, locked gazes, and put her new

sexual bravado to the ultimate test. "I want you completely naked."

Her breath whooshed out of her. So much for the slow, tantalizing seduction she'd envisioned. "You want me to get undressed?"

The barest hint of a smile played around his mouth. "Yeah, that's usually how a person gets naked."

She hesitated, feeling a twinge of uncertainty, and modesty. "What about you?"

"Anything goes, Brooke," he said, reminding her of their pact. "This is *my* fantasy. You can have yours later."

She swallowed, hard, and wondered what he intended. "And what fantasy is that?"

"There were two questions on that survey that captured my interest. Or rather, your answers did. The first question asked if you'd be open to experiencing new and different sexual positions. You said yes. Do you still feel that way now?"

She heard the subtle warning in his deep voice, but the thrill of the forbidden was too strong to resist. "Yes," she whispered. "You did say variety is a good thing."

He dipped his head to hide a grin, and a shock of black hair fell across his forehead. "So I did," he murmured. "I just want to be sure you won't object to experimenting now that we're down to the nitty-gritty."

"No," she assured him. Feeling antsy and anxious, she rubbed her damp palms down her thighs. "And the other answer of mine that intrigued you?"

"When I asked you if you'd like to have multiple orgasms, you didn't give me a straight answer." His glittering gaze was hot and intense and filled with the same raw desire pouring through her veins. "I'd like one now."

Most women are incredibly sensitive after their first orgasm, but if they relax and you touch them just the right way...

Marc's blatant, outrageous claim echoed through her, stealing her breath and making her head spin.

"Yes or no, Brooke," he asked, his voice a husky growl that rumbled seductively along her nerve endings. "It's a very easy question."

Closing her eyes, she touched her hand to the fluttering pulse in her throat, and imagined his fingers there, on her breasts, and lower...giving her more pleasure than she'd ever had in a single night, in ways she'd only entertained in her mind.

A flush stole across her face, and she lifted her lashes, meeting his smoldering gaze. "Yes, I want those multiple orgasms," she said brazenly.

"And it's my fantasy to give them to you." An incredibly sexy smile lifted his mouth. "And I want you completely naked when I touch you. Those are my terms."

A breathtaking excitement seized her as she imagined the ways he might give her that release. He was being forceful and candid, and obviously believed she wouldn't follow through with her end of the bargain...to do anything he asked.

He was wrong.

Slowly, she stood up and straightened. His gaze leisurely traveled up her legs to her face, his stare bold and earthy and unapologetically sexual. There was no mistaking what he wanted from her. And there was no doubt in her mind that she was going to give him free access to her body, and enjoy every erotic moment. She only hoped that in the end she'd walk away with her heart intact.

Taking a deep breath to banish any last doubts, she reached for the hem of her top and drew it over her head.

7

MARC BLEW OUT a harsh breath as Brooke acceded to his demand and slowly stripped off her thermal shirt, peeling away that soft, warm layer of material, baring her pale, firm breasts to his gaze. His heartbeat thundered in his chest, in his ears, and a hot rush of blood surged to his groin, increasing the pressure behind his fly.

She wasn't overly large, but perfect in size to match her slender hips and those long, shapely legs of hers encased in form-fitting thermal leggings. As he watched in silent appreciation, her breasts grew full and taut, and her rosy nipples peaked. His hands itched to plump that flesh, to draw those tight crests to his mouth and use his lips and tongue to taste her.

He remained seated, with his hands clasped over his updrawn knees, unable to believe that she was actually following through with his shocking request, which had been a sexy, shameless dare he'd fully expected her to back down from at the last minute. True, he wanted to do all those things he'd told her, but he never thought she'd allow him, or them, to go so far.

And now that she was holding up her end of the bargain, the game was over and the ultimate seduction was about to begin. He'd promised her pleasure, in a very explicit manner, and that sensual gratification was something he could deliver, even if it meant sacrificing his own physical desires in the process.

In some ways, he was grateful that he didn't have any condoms with him. Touching her so intimately was risky enough to their emotions, but he suspected being deep inside of Brooke would be too intense an experience, and more complicated than what either of them agreed to.

But, Lord, how he wanted her. More than was wise. More than was ever possible. In ways that defied his mind and the restrictions he'd put on his heart and emotions.

Their time together in this cabin would have to be enough to satisfy his craving for her.

He lifted his gaze to her softly flushed face, ready to proceed with the fantasy he'd woven. "*Everything comes off, Brooke.*"

The top dangling from her fingertips dropped to the ground, and she drew a deep breath that caused her breasts to tremble. Dampening her bottom lip with her tongue, she hooked her thumbs in the waistband of her leggings and pushed the stretchy material over her hips, then bent to drag the pants down her thighs and long legs. Straightening, she kicked them aside, leaving her clad in a pair of pink silky panties trimmed in lace. Without hesitating, she slid those off, too, and stood before him gloriously naked.

Desire gripped him hard, overwhelming him with the fierce need to possess her as *his*. She was beautifully sculpted, and he took his time looking his fill. With the firelight flickering behind her, her skin shimmered with a vibrant warmth. The hair spilling across her shoulders looked soft and feathery and golden. His gaze trailed lower, over her shapely breasts, her curved waist, then stalled at the soft curls concealing softer, sensitive folds of flesh.

He thought of all the various ways he planned to give her those orgasms, and wondered how he was going to be able to touch her, feel her response as he brought her to that exquisite peak, listen to the sexy sounds she made as she climaxed, and not embarrass himself in the process.

Gathering every ounce of willpower at his disposal, he lifted his gaze to her face. His heart squeezed tight at the barest hint of insecurity he detected in her eyes—she obviously wasn't used to being so openly scrutinized. By the time he was done with her there would be nothing left of her inhibitions.

Shifting more comfortably against the couch, he straightened his legs and widened his stance, creating a space for her in between. He crooked his finger at her, and eased the tension in the air with an irresistible grin. "Come over here and sit between my legs."

She hesitated for a split second, then glided toward him, the sway of her breasts, the sensual movements of her hips and thighs, mesmerizing him. At the last possible moment she turned around, just quick enough to give him a tantalizing glimpse of her smooth, rounded bottom, before lowering herself to the flannel sleeping bag between his spread thighs. She sat straight, not touching him, her spine too rigid.

He ran his fingers down the silky skin of her back. She shivered in response, but didn't move. "Sweetheart, in order for this to work, you're going to have to scoot closer, lean against me, and relax."

She glanced over her shoulder, the smile touching

her mouth relieving him. "It's very disconcerting to be completely naked, while you're fully dressed."

Resting his wrists on his knees, he merely shrugged. "This is my fantasy," he reminded her. Also his barrier of clothes acted as a safety precaution, a way for him to keep his perspective on the situation without losing complete control.

She settled more fully against his chest, until her buttocks nestled against his rock-hard groin. She placed her arms on his thighs, but kept her knees bent and closed primly.

That wouldn't do at all.

Gently hooking his bare feet against the inside of hers, he drew her ankles a good twelve inches apart, opening her to him, and letting the heat of the fire warm every inch of her naked flesh. She didn't resist, but the gooseflesh rising on her skin was enough to indicate her brief bout of self-consciousness.

Starting slow, he spanned her waist with his hands and brushed his fingers along her belly. She flinched at that sudden contact, and an unpredicted swell of tenderness filled his chest. Despite the sexy bargain they'd struck, he wanted this to be good for her. The best she'd ever experienced.

"Close your eyes, Brooke," he murmured, grazing his mouth against her ear. "Just focus on your body, and what you're feeling."

Listening to his advice, she let her lashes fall and relaxed her head against his shoulder. He sensed the last of her nerves drain away, and her limbs grew heavy and complacent. Taking advantage of her acquiescence, he nuzzled the side of her neck at the same time he cupped her breasts in his palms and kneaded the firm flesh. He flicked his thumbs over the nipples that had stiffened for him, then rolled those tight, velvety crests between his fingers, wishing he could do the same with his tongue.

A throaty moan purred in her throat, and she reached up and tentatively pressed her hand to his stubbled cheek. She rolled her head to the side, giving him greater access to the column of her neck, and he placed a hot, openmouthed kiss just below her ear.

She gasped, and squirmed restlessly against him. Deciding she was ready for him to move on, he flattened his palms and slid his hands down her quivering stomach then along both of her thighs, leisurely stroking the skin the fire had heated. Slowly, languorously, he petted her, drawing out the pleasure, heightening her need, strumming his fingers everywhere except where she burned the most for his touch. His thumbs met at her juncture, grazing the soft downy hair there, tantalizing her with the promise of something far more exquisite.

She turned her head toward his and opened her eyes. Her irises were a dark, aroused shade of blue, and unbridled sensuality etched her expression. "No more teasing, Marc," she said, her voice husky with impatience. "Touch me, please." Her hand slid from his cheek around to the nape of his neck. Her fingers tangled in the strands curling against the collar of his shirt, and she inexorably drew his mouth to hers. "Touch me now."

Their parted lips met, and she clung to him, drawing his tongue into her mouth. He let her dictate the pace, and followed her lead into a slow, deep, hot seduction.

One kiss melted enticingly into another, and he surrendered to the sweetness of her mouth taking his.

And then he touched her intimately, where she was wet and eager and so incredibly primed. At his first gliding stroke, her groan vibrated against his lips. After all the mental stimulation they'd endured, along with his physical caresses, he knew she was beyond ready and right on the edge. Knowing there was much more to come beyond this initial release, he didn't bother drawing this climax out, which would have been pure torture for her.

With one hand splayed on her stomach, he deepened his exploration, rubbed his callused thumb over her swollen, needy flesh, once, twice…the third time sent her straight into the realm of pleasure. Her orgasm hit her fast and furiously, the buildup so intense her entire body convulsed. She wrenched her mouth from his as a lusty cry ripped from her throat. Burying his face against her neck, he wrapped his free arm around her waist and held her as waves of pure, blissful fulfillment engulfed her.

With a final shudder and a repleted sigh, she slumped back against his chest, her breathing as ragged as his own. Though a pulsing, throbbing need settled low, Marc couldn't deny the sense of masculine satisfaction he experienced in making her come apart for him.

A log on the fire settled, sending sparks filtering up the chimney. Outside, the storm howled and snowflakes pelted the windows. Inside, they were in a world all their own, where there were no rules, or boundaries, or anything beyond their own sensual desires.

He placed a tender kiss on her temple, and watched

her mouth tip up in a positively delightful smile. "I take it that felt good?"

Her head rolled on his shoulder, and she tilted her face up to his. The wonder in her gaze did enormous things for his ego. "Mmm, that was absolutely decadent."

He chuckled and laced his fingers with hers, preparing for the next installment in his seduction. "One down, several more to go," he murmured wickedly. With her hands secured beneath his, he placed her palms on her breasts and squeezed her fingers gently around the plump flesh.

Her eyes widened. She sucked in a startled breath and resisted fondling herself. He could feel her heart beating erratically in her chest, and the pulse at the base of her throat fluttered madly. "Marc..." The tremor in her voice relayed her uncertainty.

He had no doubts that she'd touched herself before—she'd admitted as much when they'd answered those survey questions—but a certain male intuition told him she'd never done so in front of another man. Excitement escalated within him at the thought of being the first to share and witness such an erotic act.

Lifting one of her hands to his mouth, he lapped his tongue across the center of her palm and over her fingers, dampening the surface. "I want to show you how much pleasure you're capable of experiencing, all the different ways you can enjoy your body, and I don't want you to hold anything back. Be greedy, Brooke."

He dragged her slick hand back over a taut breast and administered the same provocative treatment to her other palm. She moaned and rubbed her thumbs over her beaded nipples, arching into her own touch, her reserve rapidly fading.

"Yeah, just like that," he praised, his voice thick and rough as he watched. "It's just you and me and hours stretching ahead of us. Whatever feels good, just do it."

This time around, she offered no resistance when he gently skimmed her palms lower, over her ribs and abdomen then along the inside of her thighs. Fingers still entwined, he splayed her hand at the apex of her legs and trailed her fingers along the moist, silky cleft in between.

She flinched at the direct contact, and whimpered, telling him she was still sensitive after her recent orgasm. "Soft and slow," he whispered. Determined to give her more, he directed her touch, applying a delicate, rhythmic pressure with her fingers to that responsive bud, until he was no longer instructing her and she'd found her own personal rhythm that rekindled the acute sensations.

Her face was flushed, and her hips undulated against her caressing fingers. Her breathing deepened, grew choppy, and within moments her climax beckoned.

The eroticism of the act shook Marc to the core. Feeling primitive and predatory, he filled his hands with her breasts, then bent his head and sank his teeth into the flesh between her neck and shoulder, claiming Brooke with a passionate love bite.

That's all it took to release the floodgates a second time. The breathy, intimate sounds she made nearly had him coming right along with her.

Before she had the chance to float back to earth, Marc moved around her, pulled her all the way down on the sleeping bag and straddled her hips, careful to keep his weight off her. She was weak and so dazed in the aftermath of experiencing such luxurious pleasure all she could manage was a drowsy, satisfied smile. Her hair was dishevelled around her face, and her hands rested beside her head in complete and open surrender.

Returning her smile, he gently ran his fingers over her breasts and teased the pretty tips with featherlight strokes. "Ready for more?"

She bit her bottom lip, arching restlessly into his hands and the thighs bracketing her hips. "Yeah," she said, thrilling him with her easy capitulation, and her trust.

Burning up from the inside out, he yanked his shirt over his head. Her hands followed right behind, skimming up his hard, jean-clad thighs, and fluttering over his taut belly, exploring unabashedly. Her finger dipped into his navel, then followed the dark trail of hair that whorled southward and disappeared into the waistband of his jeans. Glancing up at him with a hunger that stole his breath, she moved her flattened palm lower and massaged the fierce erection begging for freedom. Unable to help himself, he groaned and thrust against her splayed hand.

Every muscle in his body flexed and strained toward the heady, tingling sensation coursing through his blood. Knowing his control was too close to shattering, that her touch threatened his good intentions, he grasped her wrists and stretched her arms above her head.

Their faces were inches apart, and he dropped a soft kiss on her lips, then allowed a sinful grin to ease across his features. "This is where we improvise on the padded handcuffs."

Her eyes widened in surprise, but she issued no protest when he leaned over her, wrapped his shirt sleeves around her wrists, and tied the ends to the leg of the coffee table. She'd agreed to "anything goes," and he'd told her there was no saying "no," but he found himself searching her expression for the slightest hint of hesitation or objection, and found none. Her eyes were bright with anticipation, eager for whatever he had planned.

He lowered his head and started slow, with long, deep kisses that thrilled and aroused. Tongues tangled rapaciously, damp lips slid silkily, and beneath him he felt her grow lethargic and pliant. Finally, he moved on. His lips glided over her jaw, then down her throat, searing her skin and blazing a hot, moist trail to her breasts.

He brushed his lips across her nipples, teasing her, tempting him, then flicked his tongue over the stiff crown, tasting her for the first time. Her sharp intake of breath echoed in his ears, along with the whispered word *"Please."*

Lifting her breast, he enclosed her in the heat of his mouth and suckled gently, then more urgently, until she moaned long and low and writhed beneath him. She was sweet and warm and irresistible, and he couldn't seem to get enough of her.

In time, his hands and lips moved lower, scattering kisses along the slope of her belly and sampling the curve of her hip with his tongue. He made a place for himself between her legs, and with a gentle touch to her bent knees, she opened wider for him, giving him free rein to her body, and every sensual secret she harbored. His nostrils flared as her feminine scent played havoc with his senses and provoked raw, primitive instincts no other woman had ever roused in him.

The emotions caught him off guard, made what he was about to do with Brooke more than just simply satiating physical urges. *Need* consumed him. The strong, undeniable sentiment clawed at his insides, squeezed tight around his heart, making him feel desperate and impatient.

He glanced up at her face, knowing this wasn't only his decision to make. Blue eyes dark with passion boldly stared back. Without any doubts, she knew what he wanted, knew his intentions, and craved this ultimate intimacy as much as he did.

Brooke tugged on the bonds restricting her arms, aching to touch Marc. As he devoured her with his smoldering gaze, she'd never felt so vulnerable—or so connected—to a person in her life. A storm raged between them, a sensual tempest that excited as much as it frightened because she feared she wouldn't survive the emotional impact.

At the moment, none of that mattered. The ache spreading through her body couldn't be denied, nor could the soul-deep hunger he'd awakened. They'd come this far, and she'd given him everything else. He'd stolen more than any other man ever had, had given so selflessly in return, there was no reason not to trust him with this, too.

"Anything goes," she whispered, giving him the consent he sought.

He needed no more encouragement. Eyes turning slumberous, he slid even lower, curved her legs over

his broad, muscled shoulders, and settled in for an un-
hurried exploration. His dark head moved down, and
he pressed a sizzling, openmouthed kiss against the
quivering skin of her inner thigh. She gasped as his
stubble chafed her, and shivered and moaned when he
soothed the burn with his hot, wet tongue. He nibbled
leisurely on her thighs, lapped her skin, and spent an
inordinate amount of time discovering erogenous
zones she never knew she had.

She thrashed and moaned, begged and pleaded,
frustrated by her inability to thread her fingers through
his hair and direct his mouth to a more explicit kind of
touch.

But he knew. His fingers caressed her slick folds
first, seconds before his hot breath washed over her
and he laved her with the velvet heat of his tongue,
feasting on her as if she were some sweet, rare delicacy
for him to enjoy and savor.

Despite her husky pleas, and because he knew he
could, he took his time and learned everything about
her body. The feather-soft stroke of his tongue that
made her whimper, the teasing flick that drove her
mad, and the gentle suckling that pushed her closer to
the edge.

The assault became more than she could bear, and
he seemed to sense that, too. Without preamble or further preliminaries, he spread her with his thumbs and
pressed his mouth hard against her, rasping her sensitive flesh with his tongue, over and over, then delving
deeper, making love to her the only way possible. Two
fingers slipped within her tight channel, filling her,
touching off a whole new series of sensations as he
ruthlessly pushed her higher. The contractions in her

womb built, then exploded, catapulting her straight over the precipice. Her hips shot upward, and she screamed as she came in a fiery, liquid rush that shook her entire body.

With a low, primitive growl, he reared back to his knees and fumbled with the snap on his jeans, then struggled to lower his zipper over his straining sex. The muscles in his abdomen rippled with his abrupt, anxious movements, and he cursed the thermal underwear he'd put back on after his shower, which now provided a frustrating hindrance.

Startled by his abrupt change, and uncertain of what he meant to do, she attempted to capture his attention before they went further than either of them intended. "Marc?"

The caution in her soft voice was unmistakable, and he immediately lifted his head, his gaze dragging up the length of her, from her splayed thighs, to her breasts, and all the way up to the shirt that still confined her wrists. Pure, male instinct glittered in his eyes, and his chest rose and fell with deep breaths.

She drew a steady breath, though her limbs still quaked. "I thought you said you didn't have any protection with you."

He closed his eyes as a shudder wracked his body. "I don't," he said, seemingly struggling with some internal battle. When he looked at her again, his expression was a curious blend of agony and hope. "I just want to feel you against me, with nothing between us. Will you let me do that?"

Impossible as it seemed, an electrifying thrill ignited deep in her belly. She smiled invitingly, and nodded. "Yes." After everything they'd shared today, she couldn't refuse his request. Didn't want to, because she yearned to feel him, too.

She watched him shove his pants and thermals over his hips and eagerly divest himself of the restricting garments. Naked and inflamed, a gorgeous, masculine work of art, he moved over her, bracing his arms at the side of her head to support his weight. Gradually, he lowered his body...chest to lush, swollen breasts, taut stomach to plush belly, muscular legs to the welcoming cove between her thighs. Finally, he flexed his hips, nestling his arousal firmly, intimately between her legs.

They both groaned in unison at the exquisite pleasure that washed over them.

He raked his fingers through her hair, and dragged his thumb across her bottom lip. "I don't think I've ever felt anything more perfect." Awe infused his voice.

Her throat grew tight. "Me, either," she said, knowing it to be true.

He moved, sliding his hard, pulsing shaft against her slick, feminine folds. Her breathing hitched, and she arched into him.

His gaze darkened, and a cocky grin canted his mouth. "Feel good?"

"Yeah," she admitted, beyond being bashful. "For you, too?"

"Incredible." He bent his head and kissed her cheek, her jaw, then nuzzled her ear. "The only thing that could feel any better is being deep inside you."

With his words, she experienced a profound sense of emptiness, a loss she couldn't account for. "I'm sorry," she whispered.

He met her gaze and shook his head. "No apologies, Brooke. This is the next best thing." He dragged a hand down her side and cupped her bottom, tilting her hips so the next time he thrust he created a delicious, breathtaking friction.

She gasped, and he growled deep in his throat, the sound vibrating against her chest. "You're so warm, and soft, and wet." His gaze turned hot and possessive. "Move with me, Brooke. I want to feel you come, just like this."

She wriggled her hands, wanting freedom to indulge in this experience without restrictions. "Untie me, Marc. I want to touch you."

Reaching up, he slipped a finger in the knot, and the soft shirt sleeves unraveled, setting her free. With a sigh and a smile, she closed her eyes and caressed the taut slope of his back, his toned buttocks, and back up his muscular arms, learning the feel of *him*. Every time he moved, sparks of heat skittered through her, and she suddenly couldn't get enough.

Tangling her fingers in his silky hair, she brought his mouth to her parted lips and kissed him in a brazen manner that would have shocked her if he hadn't already shed her of her straightlaced demeanor. There was nothing demure left, and she reveled in the sexual abandon that was hers. Rocking with the steady movement of Marc's hips, she embraced the sheer erotic sensation of sleek, male flesh gliding provocatively along the hot, liquid center of her. Impossibly, another swell of tension coiled inside her, tighter and tighter...

With a raw curse, Marc jerked back, and Brooke mourned the loss. Before he could completely leave her, she wrapped her legs around the back of his thighs, holding him hostage.

Their harsh breathing mingled, and she ignored the savage frown creasing his brows. "Where do you think you're going?"

His jaw clenched with restraint. "I'm too close."

She caressed a hand over his cheek and smiled seductively. "So am I," she said, her meaning clear.

Despite the severity of the moment, a glimmer of amusement sparkled in his eyes. "Greedy wench."

"Your fault," she murmured. With the strength of her limbs, she drew him as close as possible, arching upward to deepen the contact, to increase the incredible friction. "You did promise me multiple orgasms, and I want them all."

A low, strangled moan caught in his throat, and he gave up the fight, surging strong and sure, and with deliberate purpose. His lips crushed hers, and he took control of their kiss, slanting his mouth over hers, again and again. Sensation spiked through her blood, centering between her legs, and she slid her body sinuously, erotically against his in a rhythm that matched the thrust of his tongue, the frenzied pumping of his hips.

Brooke's climax built, and she writhed frantically beneath him, clawing at his back to get closer. He held her mouth captive, swallowing her moans, pushing her toward yet another stunning, unparalleled peak. The feelings he evoked were too intense, too strong...and she couldn't deny the sensations that exploded within her, or her lusty response.

A guttural groan ripped from Marc's chest as he rode the crest with her, wringing every drop of pleasure from her body. At the last possible moment he raised up and over her, sliding his throbbing manhood against her soft belly. Tossing his head back, he ground his hips into her, over and over, shuddering with the violent force of spilling his own release.

He collapsed on top of her, burying his face against her neck, their damp bodies still entwined, but satiated. Closing her eyes, she wrapped one arm around his back and threaded the fingers of her other hand through his hair, absorbing his warmth, his weight, and inhaling the musky scent of their lovemaking.

A smile found its way to her lips. The heavy beating of his heart echoed hers, and the sheer magic of what they'd just shared saturated her with unbelievable contentment. Nothing had ever seemed so completely natural, so extraordinarily perfect, as this moment. A sense of rightness settled over her, as did the startling realization that the pleasure Marc had given her had not only dissolved her inhibitions, it had stripped her to the very essence of her soul.

SO MUCH FOR willpower and discipline, Marc thought, glancing down at the napping woman cuddled against his side. Obviously, he had absolutely none where Brooke was concerned, and that revelation caused a frisson of unease to sneak up on him and rattle the convictions he'd lived by for the past eight years. He'd meant to give her pleasure, and without a doubt he'd executed that plan in spades, but he'd *never* anticipated that she'd switch the tables on him and demand his own acquiescence in return.

Resisting her hadn't been an option and he'd gone wild, surrendering to the most intense, mind-blowing

orgasm he'd ever experienced. The connection between them had been extraordinary and consuming,
all without even being inside her. Incredible didn't
even begin to describe what they'd shared, and now he
was trying to sort through the conflicting, confusing
emotions that had swamped him in the aftermath of
such an amazing encounter.

The fire he'd rebuilt in the hearth after their sensual
love play snapped and hissed at the wood stacked on
the grate. A soft sigh escaped Brooke in her sleep and
she snuggled closer to him on their makeshift bed in
front of the fire. His arm automatically shifted around
her shoulders to accommodate her position and keep
the warmth of her body next to his. Her cheek rested
on his chest, her arm spanned his waist, and a slender
leg draped over his thigh, entwining their naked bodies as familiarly as the lovers they'd become.

Except he'd always steadfastly avoided this particular intimacy with the lovers he'd slept with in the past,
and for very good reason. In his experience, sticking
around after sex gave a woman the wrong impression,
and was too easily construed as an invitation to something deeper he had no intentions of offering, not when
he knew he lacked the ability to offer that kind of lasting commitment.

But instead of feeling suffocated or antsy to put distance between him and Brooke, he was filled with a
tenderness and affection that warred with the subtle
warnings slipping through his mind—that he'd fallen
deeper, and more emotionally, than he'd ever intended. He'd always secretly desired Brooke, but ac-
knowledging the awesome need she stirred was a very

dangerous thing, because nothing could ever come of it beyond their short, private time in this cabin.

No commitments, no promises and no regrets.

They'd established the terms of their brief fling before they'd crossed that line of no return. She knew up front that this was a temporary affair, that a future was impossible, and forever wasn't something he'd consider. Despite how compatible and in tune to each other they were physically, he had to believe that they'd both abide by those rules and leave this cabin without unrealistic expectations, guilt or other emotional entanglements.

She'd said no regrets, and she hadn't shown any signs of shame or doubts after they'd made love. Indeed, she'd appeared downright pleased with herself, and the lengths she'd driven him to. As for his own loss of control, that was something he'd be more careful to keep a tight rein on next time.

Snow continued to fall outside and showed no signs of stopping anytime soon. The last time he'd glanced at his watch, it had been only half past noon, with the rest of the day and night stretching ahead of them—along with tomorrow, if the storm didn't abate.

That meant long, endless hours filled with anything their imaginations might conjure. With Brooke having just discovered the sensuality that had obviously lain dormant within her, Marc had no doubt that she was far from done experimenting with him, and indulging in forbidden, innovative adventures.

The thought made him instantly hard and he entertained a fantasy or two of his own. The woman seemed insatiable, and though she'd exhibited a few reservations at first, she'd gradually blossomed, eager to learn and experience the exciting wonders of her body, and his.

She'd pushed him over the edge as no other woman ever had. Now that he knew what she was capable of, he was prepared for her brand of passion and the way she wreaked havoc with his mind. For the rest of their stay he'd give her anything and everything she asked for, and then some, but ultimately, he'd be in control of each situation—mentally *and* physically.

8

"WHAT ARE YOU in the mood for?" Marc asked.

"Just about anything you have in mind," came a throaty, feminine reply.

Marc instantly responded to the sultry invitation in Brooke's voice. His stomach clenched with need, and his body grew hard with incredible, astonishing ease. Glancing from the cupboard of canned goods, he cast his gaze over his shoulder, watching as Brooke approached from the living room. A suggestive gleam sparkled in her blue eyes, and the alluring glide of her body spoke a hedonistic language that said she was his for the taking, despite that she should have been exhausted and sexually depleted from their earlier tryst.

Her nap had obviously restored her ardor and enthusiasm.

He fought the primitive urge to haul her over his shoulder and spread her back down on the sleeping bag in front of the fire for another sumptuous feast. But since they'd skipped lunch, they needed sustenance of the nutritious kind. "I'm talking *food*, Brooke."

"So am I," she said, all innocence.

Marc knew better. With his earlier encouragement, the sensual creature within Brooke had been unleashed, and she was enjoying the benefits of being so winsome, of basking in the glory of physical liberation.

Her new, brazen attitude showed in her soft expression—the come-hither look in her heavy-lidded eyes, and the I-want-*you*-for-dinner smile curving her mouth.

No way could any healthy, red-blooded male resist that kind of ambush.

He drew a deep, steady breath to calm his raging hormones. This was a fascinating side to Brooke he'd never seen before, and he couldn't help but wonder how this sexy, exciting woman hadn't been more than enough to satisfy his brother. Obviously Eric hadn't taken the time to discover all that passion simmering beneath the surface, hadn't taken the care to coax her desires and needs to their full potential.

Or maybe Eric hadn't wanted *his wife* to be that kind of woman. The sudden, fleeting realization slipped through Marc's mind, making sense in a warped kind of way. Before he could analyze the thought further, it was quickly obliterated by the press of Brooke's body up against his chest, and the bold way she dragged her palms down his belly and tugged on the waistband of his thermals. Without hesitation, her fingers slipped inside.

Groaning deep in his throat, he grasped her wrists before she took him in her hands and erased his good intentions to make her dinner. With obvious regret, he withdrew her shameless touch. "We really do need to eat."

She buried her face against his neck and breathed deeply of his scent, then nibbled on his throat. "*You* taste good enough to eat."

Abrupt laughter escaped him. "*Food*, Brooke."

She lifted her head and looked up at him. A sigh unraveled from her, the sound rife with regret. "You're right, of course, especially since I want to make sure you've got plenty of energy for later."

He lifted a brow. "Later?"

A feline smile curved her lips. "*My* fantasy," she whispered, reminding him that she had a score to settle. "So, what are my choices? For dinner, that is."

Trying not to think of the ways she might extract her revenge, he turned back to the cupboard and perused their selection. "We've got beef stew, chicken noodle soup, or ravioli."

She reached for one of the bigger cans. "Let's go for something hearty and filling, like beef stew. It's going to be a *long* night."

He watched her sashay toward the stove, exuding too much confidence, and knew he was in big, big trouble.

They worked together to prepare dinner, all the while talking companionably. There wasn't an ounce of tension between him and Brooke after what had transpired earlier, just a special closeness that they'd never shared before. She flirted and teased impetuously, exhibiting all the unmistakable signs of a woman attracted to a man. She touched him often and with abandon, and he liked every aspect of their new, intimate relationship. Way too much. More than was wise.

They settled across from one another at the small table, along with their bowls of stew, saltine crackers, and the apple juice Brooke had found in the pantry. Nothing gourmet, but definitely a tasty and filling meal.

He picked up his spoon and pushed around the

steaming chunks of beef and vegetables, resuming their casual, easy conversation. "So, how do you think Jessica and Ryan are surviving being confined together during this storm?"

She spread her napkin on her lap and slanted him an inquisitive look. "How do you mean?"

"We've both noticed the verbal sparring and sparks flying between the two of them." He grinned. "I'm just wondering if they'll come out of this as friends or enemies."

"I'm not worried much about Jessica," she replied wryly, and bit into a saltine cracker she'd dipped into her stew. "She can definitely hold her own with Ryan, as you've seen."

He nodded. "And I can vouch for Ryan enjoying the challenge she presents."

A brief show of regret entered her eyes. "Unfortunately, that's all Jessica will ever be for him."

Curiosity got the best of him, prompting him to delve deeper into their discussion. "Why? They're obviously attracted to one another."

Her spoon stilled over her stew, and she met his gaze steadily from across the table. "Just as we are, but that doesn't mean anything will come of our attraction beyond the here and now, right?"

Marc's gut clenched. He had the distinct impression she was testing him and his answer, possibly hoping for more than they'd originally agreed to. As much as he wished he *could* promise her more than their pact as temporary lovers, he knew it wasn't possible. Not with him. And he refused to offer her false hopes.

"You're right that our time together is limited to this cabin, but our circumstances are different than theirs."

He chased that lame statement down with a long drink of apple juice, then concentrated on finishing his stew.

She had every opportunity to turn the tables on him, to confront their circumstances, challenge his excuse, but she didn't. He exhaled a breath of relief.

"Ryan doesn't stand a chance with Jessica," she replied, putting their conversation back on track. "There might be some kind of attraction between them, but he's a lawyer, and a divorce attorney at that. Those are two major strikes against him."

"What, exactly, does Jessica have against Ryan being an attorney?" He reached for a few more crackers. "And what's with Jessica's wisecracks? I've never heard such a colorful assortment of lawyer jokes."

She laughed lightly, but there was an odd tightness to the sound. "Collecting them is a hobby for her and has been since she was a teenager. As for her aversion to attorneys, well, that stems from lingering anger over our parents' divorce."

Marc didn't know much about Brooke's parents, or her past, and found himself interested in that aspect of her life. "What happened?" he gently prodded.

Her brow creased with reluctance. Setting her spoon in her nearly empty bowl, she hesitated, giving him the strong feeling that it had been a long time since she'd talked about her childhood. He waited, giving her the time she obviously needed to sort through memories.

She rewarded his patience, her release of breath seemingly releasing that tight hold on her thoughts. "Jessica was only nine when our parents separated—I was thirteen—but our father's actions made a huge impact on her. She was his little girl, and she idolized him, so when he left the family for a younger woman and filed for divorce, Jessica was just as devastated as my mother."

Finished with his meal, he pushed his dish aside. "And what about you?"

"Oh, I was definitely crushed," she admitted, absently running a finger over the rim of her glass. "But someone had to be strong and keep a level head during the separation."

So she'd been the sensible, reliable one of the trio—at a startlingly young age. "I take it the divorce was a nasty one?"

"Yeah," she said grimacing, the recollections he'd evoked obviously unpleasant ones. "Everything about the split was awful. Our mother was a stay-at-home wife, always had been, and when our father left she was forced back to work and had to keep two jobs in order to support us, which left me to take care of Jessica and basically take over our mother's duties at home."

He frowned, not caring for the image of her at thirteen, taking on the responsibilities of an adult when she should have been enjoying her teenage years. He silently absorbed everything Brooke and her sister had gone through, grasping a better understanding of Jessica's emotional state, as well as why Brooke was so sensible, levelheaded and stable. She'd had to be, for her sister's sake, and to support her mother's mental well-being, as well, he suspected.

"What about alimony and child support? Didn't that help your mother?" he asked.

"This is where the animosity toward attorneys comes in," she explained with a faint smile. "When our father walked out, he wiped out their savings account and took all the money they had. Come to find out, his new girlfriend liked pricey things and was very high-maintenance. He hired a cutthroat lawyer who had no compunction about taking advantage of my mother's emotional shock. He raked her over the coals, so to speak, and since my mother couldn't afford to hire a decent attorney, she lost everything. She was forced to sell our house, and after my father took his portion of the proceeds, my mother barely had enough to move us into a one-bedroom apartment and buy herself a used car to get her to her two jobs."

She glanced away toward the fireplace, but she wasn't done recounting her disturbing tale. "Somehow, my father got out of paying alimony, or he just didn't pay it at all. Child support payments were sporadic, and then they just stopped, as did his infrequent calls and visits." Her gaze found his again, the hurt in her eyes running deep—deeper than she allowed anyone to see, he'd hazard to guess. "It's been over thirteen years since we've seen or heard from him."

He shook his head in astonishment. "I can't imagine how things would have been if my parents had gone through something similar when my father had his one brief affair. Granted, Eric and I were eighteen and sixteen at the time, but if my parents hadn't worked through their problems and decided to make their marriage work then Eric and I would have been casualties of divorce, too."

Sighing, she stood and began stacking their dishes. "Consider yourself lucky. Your mom and dad obviously believed they had a marriage worth saving, despite your father's one indiscretion." A fond smile lifted the corner of her mouth at the mention of his parents, but he caught a brief glimpse of sadness in her eyes before she turned and moved toward the sink. "My father wasn't willing to work through the problems he'd created, or give up his new love interest. His family hadn't been a priority for him. His only concern was his own selfish wants and needs."

Marc cleared the table for Brooke while she filled the sink with hot, sudsy water, giving him a few quiet moments to reflect on the turmoil her father had inflicted on so many lives. His own father had strayed and caused Marc's mother emotional distress, but his family was fortunate in that his parents had worked hard to repair the problems in their marriage, and avoided becoming a statistic. Most couples weren't so lucky.

Marc had learned from his father's mistake, along with his own past transgression with another woman. That one incident in his life was a vivid reminder of why he avoided serious, complicated relationships. He had concrete proof that he had his father's wild blood running through his veins, just as Eric did, and he couldn't, *wouldn't*, risk the possibility of breaking a promise as sacred as wedding vows. Eric had tried, but those impulsive urges had destroyed his own marriage, had made Brooke a casualty of divorce not once, but *twice*. Yet she didn't seem to harbor any resentment.

He came up beside her and set their glasses on the counter, searching her expression. "After everything you've been through with your father, you don't seem bitter at all," he commented, fascinated by her acceptance when she had every reason to be cynical.

"I dealt with the situation differently than Jessica, and I couldn't afford to wallow in those hostile emotions." Shrugging, she pushed up the sleeves of her thermal shirt and dipped her hands into the soapy water. "I was too busy learning to cook and clean, raising Jessica for my mother, and keeping myself in school, too. I think I just came to accept the circumstances because I had no choice, but my sister was so young and my father's actions really disillusioned her."

His hand clenched into a fist against the crazy urge to reach out and touch her, to offer some kind of physical comfort for what she'd endured. He ached to pull her against him, hold her close, and give her everything she'd been denied. Except he was the last man who had the right to stake such a claim, to make promises he feared he'd break.

Instead, he reined in his desires to the best of his ability and opted for the consolation of words. "It sounds as though the men in your life haven't exactly been pillars of security, or fidelity."

Regret fluttered across her features as she scrubbed a bowl, rinsed it, then placed it on the dish rack. "Yeah, I'd hoped that my own marriage would be different from my parents, that I wouldn't get divorced." Her gaze captured his, the deepening color of blue revealing a puzzling culpability. "But honestly, I'm partly to blame for my marriage to Eric not working out."

His brows shot up in surprise, and he grabbed a terry towel to dry their dishes. "And how's that?"

"My expectations of Eric, and our marriage, exceeded what he'd been capable of giving me." Resignation laced her voice. "I should have seen that *before* the wedding, but I was so swept up in Eric's single-minded pursuit that I didn't take the time to analyze the situation, or the fact that I'd let his charm seduce me. Despite knowing about Eric's wild ways, I wanted to believe that he could be the kind of man to give me everything my own father hadn't given my mother. Like unconditional love. Respect. Security."

Something within him softened perceptively. Behind all that strength of hers hid a wellspring of vulnerabilities. "But you never had any of that in your marriage to Eric."

It was a statement, not a question, but she answered him, anyway. "No. But that doesn't mean I don't believe I can find a man who *will* give me those things. Next time, I just need to be more careful, and selective." An indulgent smile brightened her expression. "Even after everything my father put my mother through, she managed to find a terrific man who treats her like she deserves. They live in West Virginia and have been happily married for the past seven years."

He dried a bowl, then replaced it in the cupboard. "I guess it's just a matter of finding the right person."

She nodded in agreement. "Yeah, along with compromise and lots of open communication."

"Which you obviously didn't have with Eric." He knew that personal observation should have remained unspoken—the problems Brooke and Eric experienced in their relationship were none of his business—yet he wanted to know the details that had driven his brother toward other women, when his own wife should have been more than enough to satisfy him, emotionally and physically.

His comment didn't seem to bother her. "I tried to be a good wife, and I suppose in some ways Eric tried to be the kind of husband he *thought* he should be." Reaching for the pot on the stove, she submerged it in the water. "In the end, we both discovered we weren't meant to be together. I married Eric wanting a house in the suburbs, a dog, two or three kids and the whole family kind of thing. Eric *said* he wanted those things, too, but he was forcing himself into a role that didn't fit *him.*"

He frowned at her explanation. "What do you mean?"

"I think Eric married me because I was safe for him, a way for him to deny his true nature." She unplugged the sink, and stared out the window as the water swirled down the drain. It was completely white outside, the banks of snow nearly four feet high and they still had another day to go.

She transferred her gaze back to him. "There was an attraction between us when we first met, but once we got married, there was no real emotional intimacy between us. Eric played the part of a hardworking, serious husband, and he treated me like, well, a wife."

He put away the last of the clean utensils, not sure he was following her. "As opposed to?"

"A woman. A lover." She bit her bottom lip, a becoming blush spreading across her cheeks. "Eric and I...well, we never would have done the kind of things you and I did earlier. Our sex life was okay, but very predictable. Nothing hot or wild or exciting, and Eric seemed to prefer it that way. None of that really mattered to me, probably because I didn't know what I was missing."

Until now.

The tempting words hung between them, making him too aware of the sensual, sexy woman he'd had the pleasure of awakening within Brooke...and wanted to again.

He realized his earlier assumption had been correct. It wasn't as though Brooke hadn't been enough to keep Eric content, but that his brother had pegged her into a demure, domestic role that didn't include erotic intimacies. It had been Eric's way to keep his distance emotionally and maintain the stability of a proper marriage, while his affairs had offered the fantasy of hot sex.

Unfortunately, Eric hadn't realized he could have had the best of both worlds with Brooke.

Dragging a hand through her hair, she shook her head and grinned ruefully. "Where did all *that* come from?"

He hadn't meant for them to embark on such a serious conversation, but it was apparent their discussion had been good for Brooke—and very educating for him. "Sounds like you needed to let it all out."

As if she'd just realized all the personal things she'd confided about herself and her marriage to his brother, she slid a sheepish glance his way. "I've never really talked about my marriage to Eric to anyone. I adore your mother, but I'm not about to discuss Eric with *her*, and Jessica has her own opinion about the matter and is too quick to accuse instead of just listen. And I really shouldn't be discussing my relationship with Eric with you, either."

Tossing the towel aside, he leaned his hip against the counter and crossed his arms over his chest. "Nothing we talked about will go any further than this cabin," he promised.

"Thank you." She looked immensely relieved, believing his word without question, making him feel absurdly pleased that she trusted him so completely.

Tipping her head, she regarded him teasingly. "Do you charge by the hour for your therapy sessions, Mr. Jamison?"

He winked at her and grinned, liking this playful side to Brooke. "For you, I'll waive the fee."

"No, that won't do at all." A provocative gleam entered her gaze. "I don't have a whole lot of money on me, but I insist on paying up in other more *inventive* ways."

His libido twitched as she moved toward him. "Such as?"

"I think we've talked too much." Aligning her body against his, she twined her arms around his neck and brought his mouth down to hers. "How 'bout I show you?"

Her parted lips meshed with his, and she compensated him with long, rapacious kisses that threatened his sanity, made him wish for impossible things, and proved that she had plenty more newfound passion and desire to put to use.

9

BROOKE STARED at her reflection in the bathroom mirror, wondering how she'd lived her entire adult life without experiencing the freedom and abandon she'd discovered here in this cabin with Marc. Mentally, she felt alive, energetic and impetuous. Sexually, she felt liberated and unfettered, willing to explore desires and push limits that a few days ago she would have never dreamed she'd challenge.

And at the center of her transformation was a generous, selfless man who'd coaxed her to her full potential, made her feel enthusiastic and incredibly feminine. Marc helped her realize what she'd been missing for too many years, that she'd *settled* for certain things when she should have been much more selective and demanding about her needs.

She'd never resented that she'd been a good, responsible daughter, a reliable sister and a faithful, dependable wife. She'd sacrificed her childhood to take care of her family without complaint. She'd raised Jessica, doing her best to keep her out of trouble, and despite the clashes they'd had when Jessica had been a stubborn teenager, Brooke was proud of the woman her sister had become. And when she'd married Eric, she'd done so knowing on some level she'd be taking care of him, too, just as she'd mothered everyone else in her life. For as long as she could remember, she'd suppressed her own personal wants and desires for others, and had never begrudged her choices.

Until now, when she'd discovered all that she'd forsaken. Now, she had a wealth of wants and desires to make up for, and she planned to do so with Marc, who stirred passions that ran deeper than just superficial needs.

She'd once believed that Marc and Eric possessed too many similarities as brothers, the most predominant of which was the inability to nurture and sustain a committed relationship. But in the past few days she'd discovered too many differences between siblings to judge them as equals. While Eric had treated her formally, with his own reserved ideals of how a wife ought to be stereotyped, from the very beginning Marc had been warm and openly affectionate. He was sincere, honest and candid, and didn't pretend to be anything more than what he presented. Except she didn't think he gave himself enough credit for who he was—a man with a big heart, selfless intentions, and an endless capacity to care.

He'd shown her all that, and more.

Reaching for the hem of her thermal shirt, she drew it over her head and let it drop to the bathroom floor, shivering as the cold air caressed her warm skin. With cool fingers she touched the chafe marks on her neck from Marc's stubble, then followed the abrasive path down to her bare breasts, loving this newfound freedom to touch and enjoy her body, which Marc had introduced her to. Shucking convention and thumbing her nose at the restrictions that had ruled her life never felt so wonderful.

And being bad never felt so good.

Closing her eyes, she let a slow smile curl the corner of her mouth as she remembered the kiss she'd instigated in the kitchen after their serious conversation about her father and Eric. The kiss had led them to the couch, where they'd necked and petted and fondled each other like sex-starved teenagers. She'd intended to focus all her attention on Marc and test her seductive wiles on him, but he'd too easily managed to distract her. With a skillful caress, a deep, wet kiss, he'd reduced her to putty beneath his hands and mouth, making her a willing, wanton slave to his carnal desires.

He'd pleasured her, twice, and before she could regain her breath and restore her stamina to seduce *him*, he'd moved away and settled himself in front of the hearth, where he'd proceeded to add logs to the grate, then muttered the excuse of calling his secretary at home since there was no way he was going to be leaving here until Wednesday and Marlene had been expecting him back in the office tomorrow.

Clearly, that particular episode was over for him.

She'd been miffed that, while she'd been shameless and greedy in taking her pleasure, Marc clearly meant to maintain a tight hold on his own control.

Well, she planned to shatter his restraint.

While he'd been on his cell phone with Marlene, Brooke had retrieved a pillar candle she'd seen in one of the kitchen cupboards, a book of matches, and sequestered herself in the bathroom.

Now, it was time to execute *her* fantasy.

She no longer heard the deep rumble of Marc's voice as she talked to his secretary, and assumed he'd disconnected the call. Stripping off the rest of her clothes until she was completely naked, she lit the candle she'd brought with her and turned off the light, throwing the tiny room into seductive shadows and tingeing her skin with a golden, shimmering glow.

Drawing a steady, fortifying breath, she opened the door a crack, then called out, "Marc, can you come here for a sec?"

"Is everything okay?" came his concerned voice.

"I need you, please." It wasn't a lie. She needed him in ways that should have frightened her, but didn't. The connection they shared felt right, and too wonderful to question. The feelings he evoked were rich and vibrant and exciting, and while she'd come to acknowledge the gradual shifting of her emotions, she knew she had to tread cautiously with Marc, who'd built barriers against his innermost thoughts and feelings.

Ultimately, she trusted him, and knew, despite his fierce belief in no commitments, he was a man with integrity. But for some reason, he didn't see that goodness and decency in himself, believing instead that he was better off alone. Before they left this cabin, she was determined to unearth those reasons, and possibly take a huge risk of her own.

She heard him padding across the living room, then the door pushed open and he appeared, as did an instantaneous frown when he saw that she was naked. "What's wrong?"

"I need someone to scrub my back." Smiling invitingly, she crooked her finger at him. "Come inside and close the door."

A rush of breath escaped him. "Brooke—"

"Anything goes," she interrupted, not allowing him

the chance to refuse her, or turn the situation around so he was the one in charge again. "I've done everything you've asked me to. Now it's time for you to return the favor."

He conceded by stepping closer and shutting the door, cocooning them in flickering, soothing candlelight. "You mean to tell me you want *more* after what we just did on the couch?" His tone was amused and incredulous at the same time.

"Oh, yeah, a *whole* lot more. I'm making up for everything I've missed. And I've missed an awful lot, as you know." Her lashes fell to half-mast. "Since I plan to get you *very* wet, you need to take off your clothes."

He groaned at the provocative slant to her words. "Are you gonna help?"

She shook her head, shivering as her silky hair swayed around her shoulders, brushing her sensitive skin. "Nope. I'm going to watch you while you strip, and enjoy myself, so make the most of it."

He chuckled as he pulled his shirt over his head, and though the sound was strained with desire, the depths of his eyes glimmered with too much confidence. Brooke knew if she wasn't careful and didn't stay on guard, he'd steal this seduction right out from under her and make it his own—with her acquiescence being the ultimate prize. While she certainly didn't mind being the recipient of the luxurious pleasure Marc so easily wove, she wanted him to let go again, physically and emotionally, as he had the first time they'd made love.

"Don't be so cocky, Jamison," she murmured as he pushed his thermal pants over his hips and down his muscular legs, then stepped from the nubby fabric, completely at ease with his own nudity. And why not, when he had a magnificent body? "This time, it'll be *you* begging, not me."

He stood in front of her, large and gorgeous and every inch male, including that arrogant grin on his face illuminated by the candle's glow. "I'll certainly enjoy your attempts."

She rolled her eyes and pushed aside the shower curtain to turn on the hot water. "Has anyone ever told you that you're way too presumptuous?"

"Has anyone ever told you that you have a nice ass?" His cool, callused palm stroked her bottom, sending a wave of gooseflesh rising across her skin.

"You're the first," she said, straightening, then cast him a playful frown. "And keep your hands to yourself. This is *my* fantasy."

"Don't you think I know what really turns you on?" he asked, his rich voice infused with unwavering certainty.

He knew too much, every wanton desire even *she* hadn't known she possessed, and intimate secrets she'd never shared with anyone else. She wanted the same from him. "Well, maybe it's my turn to discover what turns *you* on."

"That's easy," he murmured as his gaze drifted down the length of her, lingering on feminine dips and curves along the way. "You turn me on."

That much was obvious by his body's reaction to her. His arousal grew full and thick, and she hadn't even touched him yet. The knowledge bolstered her confidence, made her feel *very* sexy, restoring her determination not to lose her advantage in this seduction.

"Sweet-talking me isn't going to work." Stepping

beneath the hot, steaming spray, she grabbed his hand and pulled him in. He followed willingly, but she didn't trust the wicked gleam in his eyes and knew maintaining control would be a challenge in itself.

Intending to emerge the victor this time, she closed the curtain and drenched herself from head to toe, letting him watch as the water slicked back her hair, then sluiced over her taut breasts, her belly, and down her thighs, until her entire body glistened wetly. Then she pushed him beneath the shower and let him do the same while she poured shampoo into the palm of her hand.

The fiberglass stall was small, which made for more intimate contact, and amusing and innovative ways to get clean. Their laughter and chuckles mingled as she scrubbed his hair and he did the same for her, then they helped one another rinse, chasing the suds down their limbs with slick palms. Their bodies brushed erotically, glided silkily, turning their frolicking fun into sizzling arousal and excruciating awareness.

Soft sighs and low groans coalesced. Lips met, damp and soft and hot. Their tongues tangled with delicious indulgence while her soapy hands slid over sleek sinew, discovering fascinating male contours, both hard and soft but undeniably virile.

Hunger and need coiled deep within Brooke as long, callused fingers touched and teased and tormented. Her mind spun, her pulse raced, and just when she made the silent decision to do some exploring with her mouth, he broke their kiss and eased her around so her bottom tucked against his groin and his throbbing erection nestled between her thighs.

Her breath hitched in her throat and a rush of liquid

heat greeted the sleek glide and subtle pressure of his arousal *there*. Realizing this position put *her* at *his* mercy, she tried to turn to face him again, but he snagged a muscular arm around her waist, holding her secure and tight against his heaving chest. He stepped back, until the hard, warm stream of water hit her thighs, heightening the ache between her legs, and deeper inside.

On a soft cry, she arched her back, sliding her hips intimately closer to his, but still feeling too empty. She'd sworn she wouldn't be the one to beg this time, but the need he evoked was too great, and she was helpless to deny what she wanted so badly. She craved not only physical fulfillment, but a spiritual, emotional connection that threatened the rules they'd established for their brief affair.

Turning her head, she looked up into his face, clenched with restraint, and widened her stance for him. "I want to feel you inside me, just like this." Her voice quivered, as did her whole entire body.

He pushed forward as if he couldn't help himself, creating a breathtaking friction. She gasped, and he shuddered, his expression agonized. "We can't, Brooke. I won't put you at risk that way."

Frustration blossomed within her. She wanted to argue that this was another way for him to remain dominant and disciplined with her, but how could she when his reasons were solid and rational? As much as her feelings for him were becoming deeper and more serious than she'd anticipated, an unplanned pregnancy was a complication neither of them were prepared to handle.

Her thoughts scattered the moment he slid his hand

low, spread her with his fingers, and the shower jet made a direct hit on swollen, sensitive flesh. Her knees buckled, but he held her secure in his embrace. His breath was hot on her neck, as sporadic as her own.

And then he filled her the only way he could, two fingers burrowing incredibly deep while the rhythm of his stroking thumb and the tantalizing spray of the water sent her careening swiftly over the edge. She soared straight in the realms of an explosive orgasm that sapped her of energy and strength.

When it was over, she turned in Marc's arms and sagged against his chest for support. One arm curled around his neck, and the other pressed against the strong beating of his heart.

Lifting her heavy head, she glanced up at him, her backside tingling from the pelting water. "You did it again," she accused.

"What? Made you come?" That cocky grin of his reappeared.

Unable to help herself, she laughed, surprised that she was comfortable enough with Marc to indulge in humor after sex. It was a new experience for her, and she liked it. "That, and you're not allowing yourself to enjoy the moment and just let go."

"I already had my fantasy. This one was yours." He dragged his thumb along her jaw, his touch infinitely gentle. "Besides, I enjoy watching you. Immensely."

Her face flushed at the reminder of her abandon. "It's not the same thing, and you know it." She wouldn't be deterred from her original purpose. "You're holding back, and I want to know why."

She felt him stiffen, and his heart thudded beneath her palm. "I'm not holding anything back," he said evenly, though his shadowed gaze contradicted his words.

Her eyes narrowed on him. While she'd opened up and revealed emotional, personal, intimate secrets, he was very stingy in reciprocating. He was afraid, of giving too much, of needing much more in return. She knew, because she felt it, too, and was just as scared, but was prepared to accept the possibility of something more.

Shifting against the fiberglass wall under her scrutiny, he grasped the hand resting on his chest and guided it downward, over his lean belly and lower— his purpose, she knew, to divert her barrage of questions.

He curled her fingers around his pulsing shaft, and dipped his mouth near her ear. "Here, I saved this just for you."

Oh, he was so bad, and so, so *good*. How could she resist such a gift? She stroked him lightly, feeling him grow in her palm, and marveled at the heat and size and strength of him. Rubbing her breasts against his chest, she looked up into his eyes. "How do you like it?"

"Tight. Slow and easy," he murmured. "And we've got wet covered." Fisting his hand over hers, he showed her the rhythm that turned him on the most, and she learned quickly.

With sinuous movements, his hips undulated, and he groaned low and deep at the pressure and friction they created together. "Yeah, just like that," he said huskily.

His head fell back against the wall, and she placed openmouthed kisses on his neck and shoulder. Experimentally grazing her thumb over the tip of his penis, she gleaned a slick pearl of moisture that made her eager to discover his taste and essence, to offer him the kind of mindless pleasure he'd so selflessly given her. She wanted to show him how much he'd come to mean to her with that gesture. That what they were experiencing together, no matter how fleeting, was special.

Dipping her knees, she slid her lips across his nipple, flicked her tongue over his wet abdomen, lapped the trickle of water that streamed lower...

Seemingly realizing her intent, he cursed and grasped her arms, hauling her back up before she could take him in her mouth.

She frowned at him, startled by the flare of panic that etched his features. "Marc..."

He shook his head in denial, but there was no disputing the stark need burning in the depth of his eyes, the same sentiment that clutched at her heart. Crushing his lips over hers, he swallowed her protest, attempting to drive his own fear far, far away.

She wanted to reassure him, let him know that he wasn't the only one swamped with confusing emotions, but there was no stopping the demands of his body. His thrusts quickened against her grip, and his breathing grew choppy. His hips bucked, the muscles along his stomach and thighs clenched, and then he climaxed—long, hard and furiously.

The empty sensation that settled in the pit of Brooke's stomach didn't completely surprise her. Neither did the sting of frustration. He'd given her incredible pleasure, and she'd driven him to his own release...all on his terms. Despite her best efforts, he'd maintained ultimate control.

The water continued to rain down upon them, and a shiver coursed through her. He wrapped his arms around her back, warming her skin but not her soul.

"The water is getting cold," he said after a long, quiet moment had passed. He shut off the valve and opened the curtain, which made her even chillier.

Grabbing one of the fluffy towels she'd set on the counter earlier, she handed it to him, then retrieved the other for herself. "Let's go out by the fire where it's warm," she suggested, as she towel-dried her wet hair. "I'm not done with you yet."

Doubts and an unmistakable reserve dropped over his features, as if he dreaded the possibility of her pursuing the silent conversation that had transpired between them minutes ago. She did plan to find out what kept him and his emotions at arm's length, but not tonight, when he was already on the defensive.

Turning on the light, she blew out the candle and smiled at him as she wrapped her towel around her chest and tucked the end between her breasts. "I was thinking of giving you a nice, long massage, and you can repay the favor by cuddling with me." Nothing threatening at all, just lots of intimacy she hoped to use for emotional artillery later.

A hint of a smile lifted his mouth. "Sounds like a fair trade."

"I think so." Taking his towel from him, she slung it around his waist and secured the end at his hip. "Don't bother putting any clothes on. You go build another fire, and I'm going to see if I can find some lotion to use."

With a nod, he left. She perused the items in the medicine cabinet, but didn't find what she was searching for. There were various toiletries beneath the sink, and just as she reached for a bottle of moisturizer, she knocked over a small, flat rectangular box and read the universal word Trojan emblazoned across the front. She picked up the carton, turned it upside down, and a foil packet fell into her hand.

A single condom. Feeling giddy at the resource she'd discovered, and the ammunition it provided toward shattering Marc's control, she decided to save her treasure for a very special moment. She knew exactly where she'd hide the prophylactic, so it would be handy and nearby when she needed the protection.

An elated smile spread across her face. When the time came, none of Marc's excuses would suffice, and he wouldn't be able to deny her.

10

ANOTHER NIGHT HAD PASSED with Brooke, and Marc was barely hanging on—to his rapidly slipping control, his valiant intentions and his conflicting emotions. All were conspiring against him, and like a man sinking with no life preserver in sight, he was struggling to keep a firm grip on reality—which meant no future with Brooke, no matter how much he was beginning to wish otherwise.

He *had* to keep that fact in mind, along with maintaining a clear division between fantasy and reality, despite how difficult she was making it for him. Physically, separating himself from her was easy, since they weren't going to make love in the traditional sense. Emotionally, he didn't think he'd ever be able to isolate himself from her, not when everything about her was indelibly etched in his mind. Especially the way she'd looked at him in the shower last night when he'd stopped her from taking her caresses one step further. Too many expectations had shone in her eyes, coupled with a longing that exceeded the hot, wild fling they'd agreed to.

The anxiety he'd experienced in that moment had shaken him to the core, because he'd had the overwhelming urge to just let go and give Brooke everything she wanted, everything she demanded. But the fear of ultimately hurting her later, of not being able to give her everything she deserved, of breaking promises he had no right making, kept him from letting her lavish that particular intimacy on him. He'd felt vulnerable enough without surrendering to her silent supplication to accede to *her*.

"Your turn, Jamison," Brooke said.

Squinting at the cards fanned in his right hand, he tried to concentrate on the game of Rummy they'd been playing for the past hour. He was losing, which wasn't a huge surprise—he'd lost every game they'd played so far with the deck of cards she'd discovered in one of the kitchen drawers, from poker, to crazy eights, to twenty-one, and now this.

And still, the rest of the afternoon and evening stretched ahead of them.

They'd slept in late that morning, almost to noon, and after waking up and verifying that the storm hadn't passed through yet, Brooke had coaxed him back beneath the warmth of the covers so she could snuggle with him a little longer. Their cuddling had been very relaxing and satisfying, and surprisingly, had remained platonic. The contentment and rightness of waking up with Brooke was unlike anything he'd ever experienced, and something he knew better than to get attached to.

They'd talked about inconsequential things while they lay entwined, sharing favorite movies, foods, activities, likes and dislikes, and they discovered they had a lot more in common than either of them realized. While idly skimming his hand down her side, he'd found a ticklish area right at the curve of her buttocks that sent her into a fit of gasps and giggles when he added a tantalizing pressure to that direct spot. Finding that sensitive region had been purely an accident, but one he couldn't resist exploring further, making her writhe and squirm until she breathlessly pleaded for him to stop the torment.

He did, only to have her grab a pillow when he wasn't looking and pummel him over the head. With a low growl he'd tackled her to the sleeping bag, seen the mischievous glint in her eyes, and seconds later found himself embroiled in a pillow fight. They'd rolled around naked, the moment playful and teasing and filled with raucous laughter and shrieks of indignation—until he'd rolled to his back to escape her and she'd leapt on top of him, straddling his hips to hold him down.

All teasing and fun ceased, and the pillow she'd raised to gain retribution fell to her side. The mischief in her expression faded, replaced with a soft, sensual look he was coming to know too well, and a wanting that stirred his soul. Slowly, she'd splayed a hand on his chest and dragged her palm down his belly toward her spread thighs, until her fingers met the moist heat and silken skin trapping him, teasing him, tempting him. All she had to do was lean forward, slide lower, and she'd impale him right at the heart of where he wanted to be. The urge to touch her, fill her, was so strong his blood had roared in his ears.

What is your favorite sexual position?

I like being on top.

He didn't like it. Not at all. He'd felt vulnerable under her spell, her feminine power stripping away the tenacious hold he had on his control until the only thought filling his head was being deep, deep inside her and forgetting everything else...like that he was all wrong for her.

She'd bit her bottom lip and glanced toward the couch for some unexplainable reason, as if debating what to do and how to handle their current predicament.

His stomach chose that moment to growl, loudly, obnoxiously, declaring that he'd missed breakfast and it was past time to eat. Much to his relief *and* disappointment, she'd relented to his belly's hungry demand and moved off him, though there was a look in her eyes that proclaimed she'd only given him a brief reprieve.

Marc grunted to himself. She had no clue how close she'd been to his complete capitulation.

She peeked at him from above her cards, amusement dancing in her eyes. "Does that grunt mean you're holding a lousy hand?"

"Like that should surprise you," he muttered. Picking a card from the stack, he discarded the five of hearts, then winced when he realized he'd just given away the card he needed to complete a run.

Without hesitation, she retrieved his card and tucked it into her hand, then tossed out one she didn't need and he couldn't use. "You know, you're not providing much in the way of friendly competition." And she seemed delighted that she had him completely distracted, the little minx.

Other than that one incident earlier, they hadn't touched or kissed or indulged in any more fantasies. After eating a combination lunch and dinner of ravioli, they'd each taken a shower, alone this time. While she'd been in the bathroom, he'd checked in with Marlene and made a call to the ranger station for a weather update. He'd confirmed that the storm would be gone by late that night, and was told they'd send someone out in the morning to pick them up when the roads were clear.

They had all evening and night, and so far, not one sexual advance. Although she'd been on her best behavior since that pillow fight, he didn't trust her demure act and was prepared for a surprise attack...along with a bold attempt to maintain control of whatever erotic scheme she conjured up.

"I hate to do this to you again," she said, spreading her hand out on the coffee table with a triumphant grin. "Rummy."

Rolling his eyes, he tossed his cards onto the pile. "I give up. My pride can't take any more abuse."

Laughing throatily, she crawled around the coffee table toward him. "Aww, poor baby," she crooned. "Maybe I can help soothe that male pride of yours."

He eyed her gradual approach, unable to miss the wicked, purposeful gleam lighting her blue eyes, or the anticipation curling deep in his belly. "What, you're gonna let me win the next hand?"

She lifted a blond brow. "*Giving* you the win wouldn't be any fun, now would it?" Settling onto her knees in front of where he sat on the middle of the couch, she held his gaze. "No games this time, Marc. We only have this last night left together, and I want to make the most of it."

Suddenly, so did he. As selfish as it was, he wanted what he could take from her, one last time. "Come up here on the couch," he said huskily, wanting her at eye level and within touching distance.

She shook her head and pulled off her thermal top.

Her breasts were already swollen, her nipples tight. "I'm fine where I am, thank you," she countered politely, keeping things *her* way and not allowing him any advantages. "Take your shirt off for me."

Dragging the hem up and over his head, he tossed the thermal aside, baring his chest. He watched her stand and shed her bottoms and panties, then kneel again, grasping the waistband of his long underwear. "Now let's get rid of these."

He lifted his hips as she tugged and removed the last barrier of clothing. Pressing her hands to his knees, she widened his legs and moved in between that cove, and leaned more fully into him, so his thighs bracketed the sides of her ribs and her breasts rubbed against his taut belly. She reached up, curled a hand around the back of his neck, and pulled his mouth down to her parted, waiting lips and kissed him, slow and deep, and decadently sensual. She initiated an unrushed, seductive journey of lips and tongue, as if they had the rest of their lives together, rather than just this last night.

The thought made him desperate to touch her, to memorize the feel of her, the sweet, giving taste of her mouth, the texture of her skin—for all those long, lonely nights ahead. He trailed his hands over her shoulders and along her smooth, silky back, pulling her closer still, but not near enough, not deep enough, not intimate enough. His sex pulsated between them, burning with the need to be a part of Brooke in ways that he knew were impossible—for so many reasons.

Her lips left his, trailing kisses along his jaw, the stubble long since softening to a two-day beard, then she nuzzled his neck and inhaled deeply of his scent. Her hands charted a path down his chest, and her mouth followed leisurely behind. Fingers grazed his nipples seconds before she tasted him with a wet lap of her tongue. He groaned and closed his eyes as she teased him with her lips, tantalized him with her teeth, then continued on her descent, tormenting him with the erotic feel of his erection sliding between the warmth of her breasts as she lavished attention on his belly, his navel, and the point where hip met thigh.

Then she surrounded the hard length of him in both hands, and knowing what she meant to do, he tangled fistfuls of her soft hair in his fingers and gently held her intentions at bay. His heart raced, and he battled with the urgent, excruciating need ripping through him.

She looked up at him, her eyes glazed with desire, her expression as vulnerable as he felt. "Tonight, don't tell me no," she whispered, a desperate quality infusing her voice. "I want to share this with you, *please*."

He knew what she wanted, his complete and total surrender, and there was no denying her, or himself, this intimate pleasure. This time, when she lowered her head, parted her lips over the tip of him, he didn't stop her, resigned to giving her this final fantasy and letting her have her way with him.

He watched her through heavy-lidded eyes, but was unprepared for the wild, primitive onslaught of need that gripped him when the wet heat of her mouth enveloped him. He sucked in a sharp, swift breath as fiery hunger ripped through his body. He shuddered as she stroked him rhythmically, the silky textures of her lips and tongue heightening the incredible sensations. And because there was nothing else he could do, he tightened his fingers around the silky strands of her hair and rode with the exquisite pleasure, until it became too much to bear and his release beckoned.

He swore, and pulled her away before he climaxed, feeling the loss as acutely as the frantic beating of his heart. Breathing hard, he flung his head against the back of the couch and squeezed his eyes shut, trying to regain a semblance of control.

He heard a crinkling sound, felt Brooke's fingers brushing over his fierce erection, then something tight sheathing him. Frowning, he glanced down to find her rolling a condom over his straining shaft.

He choked on hoarse, disbelieving laughter. "Where in the hell did that come from?"

A sultry smile curved her lips as she finished her seductive task. "I had it tucked between the cushions. I found one in the bathroom last night and I was saving it for the perfect moment."

The moment *was* perfect, *too* perfect, rich with possibilities, and swirling with the dangerous prospect of going all the way with Brooke, of consummating emotions he'd spent the past two days avoiding and denying.

She crawled on top of him, straddling his waist. Her slick wetness grazed him, and he grasped her hips before she could take him inside her.

He gritted his teeth against the instinctual urge to drive within her in mindless abandon. "God, Brooke, are you sure about this?" he asked, his voice low and rough. "*Really* sure?" He had to know, because once they made love, there would be no retracting the intimate act...and no experiencing it again.

Like the condom, this was a one-shot deal, reserved for this time in the cabin only.

Framing his face between her palms, she gazed into his eyes, searching so deep he could swear she could see straight to his soul. "I've never been more sure of anything in my whole entire life."

Neither had he. But that changed nothing. "No regrets tomorrow?"

She shook her head, graceful and beautiful and certain. "Never."

"No promises?" He forced the words out around the painful vise tightening his chest.

Her fingers slipped into his hair, curved around the nape of his neck, and she smiled. "Just the promise of pleasure."

The last rule got stuck in his throat, and he felt as though he'd ripped out a piece of his heart when the words finally emerged. "No commitments?" He had to make sure she understood and agreed.

She didn't answer, and instead kissed him, contradicting his final stipulation with so much passion and emotion he was helpless to resist her, despite what her eloquent silence had stated.

She wanted what he couldn't give.

"Make love to me, Marc," she breathed against his lips, and reached down to surround him with hungry hands, guiding him toward the heart of her. "I need you."

The honest statement tore at his resolve, shattered his restraint. There was no denying this woman, or the powerful longing she evoked. He was too far gone, beyond reasoning. He was hers for the taking, a willing partner in this primitive desire to mate and be one.

With a shivery little sigh, she sank down on him, flowing over him like honeyed heat. With a deep, guttural groan, he thrust upward, burying himself to the hilt in her sleek warmth. Too many heartbeats to count passed as they absorbed the feel of one another. Then they gradually began the sinuous movements and gliding rhythm of two lovers completely in sync.

With the intensity of the emotions swirling between them, he expected wild and rushed. She gave him slow and tantalizing, drawing out this one and only joining for as long as possible, taking as well as giving. Threading her fingers through his hair, she tugged his head back, leaned into him, and brushed her nipple across his lips. He took her into his mouth, suckling her breast, nipping gently, lapping indulgently, greedily feasting on the sweet taste of her.

It wasn't enough. Not nearly enough. His hands grew restless, and he filled his palms with her soft, supple flesh, caressing her spine, across her buttocks, along her gently rocking hips. He skimmed his fingers down the length of her sleek thighs, then back up again, grazing his thumbs where their bodies joined, pleasuring her with an illicit, knowing touch.

Her breathing deepened, and he looked up into her flushed face, met her drugged gaze, and knew he was lost.

Possibly forever.

Knowing he wouldn't last much longer, he increased the pressure to that pulse-point of hers, building the tension they'd kept harnessed for too long, until her ragged breathing indicated just how close she was to that sharp edge.

Taking hold of her hips, he surged powerfully, filling her completely, again and again, until his thrusts turned into an uncontrollable extension of his need for her.

Rapture finally swept her up in its wild, tempestuous current. He heard the excitement of it in the moan that escaped her throat, saw the thrill of it in her eyes before they rolled back in ecstasy, felt the elation of her abandon in the way her body arched toward his and her inner muscles clenched so exquisitely around him.

But it was his name on her lips as she reached that crest that unraveled his control, shattered his restraint, and made him shudder with the incredible force of his own release.

And this last time, he came with her, and held nothing back.

STANDING BY the cabin's front window, Marc stared out at the blackness that had descended with the onslaught of midnight, no longer glimpsing the occasional glow of snowflakes drifting by the glass pane. The storm outside had finally passed through the Rocky Mountains. He wished the upheaval within him would abate just as completely.

Unfortunately, he suspected the memory of these past two days with Brooke would haunt him for the rest of his lonely, solitary life.

He scrubbed a hand down his face, unable to stop thinking of the woman he'd left sleeping on their bed in front of the dying fire, soft and warm and replete from their lovemaking. An occasional cold draft drifted his way from the covered hole in the window, but it wasn't enough to numb him—his mind, his body, or the pain in his heart. It ached with wanting Brooke. Stung with the knowledge that the one woman he craved in ways even *he* didn't understand could never, ever be his...not in that deep, intrinsic way that mattered most.

Unease tightened his belly. When had those emotional issues started to make a difference to him? And how in the hell had he allowed Brooke to breach barriers and convictions he'd erected after discovering he was a man who lacked the ability to commit? For the past eight years he'd effectively dodged romantic entanglements and intimate relationships, and poured most of his time and energy into building his business. No single woman had distracted him from his goals and personal creed to embrace bachelorhood. No one woman had tempted him to question his vow to live a solitary life.

Until Brooke. She inspired tenderness and affection. She roused passion and desires he never knew possible. She kindled a hunger that surpassed anything he'd ever imagined, or felt. She provoked needs that sex alone couldn't quench. In just one wonderful weekend she'd dragged him deeper than he'd ever gone with any woman.

And he had no idea what he was going to do about her hold over him once they left this cabin.

"Marc?"

Brooke's sleep-husky voice drifted from behind him, and he glanced her way. She'd propped herself up on her elbow, and her disheveled hair spilled over her bare, smooth shoulders. The blanket slipped low, revealing perfect breasts tipped with taut, rosy nipples. There wasn't a hint of inhibition about her now, and he loved that about her, and that he was directly responsible for her sensual transformation.

Love. The word surged through him like a 220-volt shock, paralyzing him on many levels. Denials came swiftly, and he grasped each one, using them as a means to shore that unexpected flood of emotion.

It couldn't happen.

She tipped her head, her brow creasing with concern. "Are you okay?"

No, he didn't think he'd ever be the same again. "I'm fine." His voice cracked, and he swallowed hard to clear it.

"Come back over here." She patted the space beside her. "It's getting cold and I miss you."

His chest tightened. *He was going to miss her, too.* Forcing the thought from his mind, he moved across the room, irresistibly drawn to her.

"You put your thermals back on," she complained with an adorable pout when he neared. "Take them off."

"Yes, ma'am." He shucked his underwear, and she lifted the blanket for him to slip inside next to her. She turned so he could spoon his body along the back of hers—wanting nothing from him but to simply be held.

And he did just that, all night long—it would be his last chance to do so.

11

SHE'D BROKEN their rules, Brooke acknowledged the next morning as they attempted to restore the cabin to its original order. While she harbored no regrets for what she and Marc had shared in this cabin, she'd discovered that she wanted promises from Marc. But she also knew she had no right to ask for something more lasting and definite, not when he'd made his terms of this affair abundantly clear from the very beginning.

No commitments. And because she'd openly agreed to that condition, she had to respect the pact they'd made and let him go, no matter how much her heart wished otherwise.

Straightening the place mats on the table, she slanted a glance at Marc, who was folding the blankets in the living room while she cleaned up the kitchen. Outside, she could hear the snowplows clearing the roads. Within the next hour, someone from the ranger station would be there to pick them up, retrieve their snowmobile, and take them back to their place.

Their chores gave Marc the perfect excuse to avoid her. All morning, he'd kept his distance, keeping conversation to a minimum and physical contact nonexistent. It was as though he'd shut down in the hours before dawn. She'd thought, *hoped*, that their intimate lovemaking the night before had breached the barriers between the flirtatious, carefree man she'd always known, and the caring, complex man she'd glimpsed here in this cabin. She was wrong.

When she'd embraced the idea of an affair with Marc, she hadn't considered anything more than the pleasure, fantasies and fun she'd requested. One wild fling to enjoy and savor before returning to her responsible job as an accountant, and her staid, predictable life. He'd given her all those thrills she'd sought, and so much more. But she'd never expected to discover herself as a woman because of Marc's coaxing, never expected to feel so liberated and free.

And she never, *ever*, expected to fall in love with him.

The realization didn't send her into a panic like it would have a week ago, just as she'd panicked the night he'd kissed her at his parents' anniversary party. Ever since that evening, she'd been struggling against the inevitable, denying what had been so patently obvious in that magical embrace. There was a chemistry between them, an instantaneous connection that transcended sex or lust and touched on something special. She knew Marc had felt it, too, despite his current aloof attitude.

Finished wiping down the kitchen counter, she rinsed the dish rag, drew a deep, fortifying breath...and finally broke the strained silence between them. "Since we've made ourselves at home here, we'll have to find out who owns this cabin so we can reimburse them for our stay, and for the damage to their front window."

"I'm sure the ranger station can help with that information." He rolled up a sleeping bag and secured it

with the ties, keeping his gaze on the task. "I'll take
care of everything when I get back to the office later today."

His business could have waited a day or two for his
return, but she knew he was grasping any excuse to
put distance between them. Clearly, he had no inten-
tion of pursuing her beyond today, and that knowledge hurt in ways she doubted would ever heal.

Struggling to keep her own emotions under wraps,
she put the last of their breakfast dishes away. "I'll split
the cost with you, so be sure to let me know what I
owe."

He glanced at her, his frown fierce. "*I'll* pay for it."

His insistence on footing the bill made her curious
about his reasons, and provoked her to find out. Deem-
ing the kitchen spotless, she headed toward the couch,
stopping behind it. "Are you insisting on taking care of
any charges because you want to, or are you doing it to
ease your conscience?"

He jerked his head back up again, and glared at her.
The short, dark beard lining his jaw added to his
brooding appearance and made his eyes a piercing,
glittering shade of gray. "What the hell is that supposed to mean?"

She crossed her arms over her chest, refusing to allow his gruff tone to discourage her. "You're feeling
guilty."

The muscles beneath his shirt tensed, and he immediately averted his gaze to the other sleeping bag, con-
firming that her suspicions had been accurate. Relief
poured through her. His guilt, no matter how mis-
placed, meant that he cared about her. It wasn't a dec-

laration of his feelings by any stretch of her imagination, but it did give her a slim glimmer of hope.

Then he crushed her optimism with his next announcement. "I'm thinking that maybe this wasn't such a good idea."

She knew without asking what "this" referred to. Them. Together. Intimately. "Kinda late for second thoughts or *regrets*, don't you think?" she said, referring to the conditions he'd insisted on.

He winced, but didn't back down from his own personal crusade to dissuade her. "Yeah, I suppose it is." Scooping up the blankets topped with their pillows, he turned and headed up the loft stairs, effectively severing their discussion.

Easing out a taut stream of breath, she took her aggravation out on straightening the sofa cushions. Unfortunately, touching the couch only served to remind her of the passion that had consumed them last night when they'd made love, his needy response to her aggressive approach, the desperation in his touch, and the emotion in his ultimate surrender. What had transpired between them was rare and wonderful and unique, and for some people, a once-in-a-lifetime opportunity. Having experienced a monotonous, passionless relationship with Eric, and having witnessed her own parents' desolate marriage, she refused to settle for less than mutual desire, excitement, and soul-deep devotion.

She and Marc had experienced all three, so why couldn't he admit that what they'd shared was worth exploring beyond today?

She watched him descend to the lower level and cross the room to the fireplace. Removing the screen, he prodded the logs with the poker, making sure that all the embers had burned out. His movements were brusque and filled with restless energy.

She resisted the urge to come up behind him and knead her fingers along the taut sinew bisecting his spine. Certain he wouldn't welcome her touch—not when he was using that tension surrounding him as armor—she kept her hands to herself.

Dragging her fingers through her hair, she stared at his back and continued the conversation he'd tried to divert minutes ago. "Are you going to tell Eric about us being stranded together?"

He hesitated for a few heartbeats. "Yeah." His tone was gruff, but resigned. "I'm sure he'll find out about it one way or another, since he knows Ryan and Shane. It's best if the news comes directly from me so he doesn't think we're hiding something."

She bit her lip to keep from reminding him that they *were* hiding something—the fact that they'd had a wonderful, thrilling affair. "Will you tell him about *us?*" she asked, more pointedly this time.

He shook his head, and kept jabbing the ashes in the grate. "I don't think our being together, or what we did in this cabin, is anyone's business but our own." Setting the poker back in its brass stand, he replaced the screen, giving the task way too much attention.

Resting her bottom on the couch's armrest, she wondered if there would always be this awkward tension and unease between them now. She wanted to know what to expect from Marc in the future when they encountered one another at his mother's house, which was bound to happen sooner or later.

She voiced her concern. "What about us seeing one another?"

Finally, he turned around and faced her, his expression a heartbreaking combination of anguish and fierce control. "I don't do relationships, Brooke," he said roughly. "Nothing long-term or serious. You knew that going into this affair."

He'd misunderstood her question, but that didn't stop her heart from giving an odd little twist. She couldn't refute his claim. He *had* warned her, and she'd blindly agreed to his terms. But that had been before she knew an affair with him would alter her expectations, and make him one of the most important people in her life. Unfortunately, he didn't want to be a part of hers.

Very calmly, she replied. "All I meant was that I'm sure we'll run into one another at some point. Thanksgiving is coming up, and you know your mother usually invites me over since my mother lives out of the state. Is that going to be a problem for you?"

He thought about that for a quiet moment, and it was obvious to her that he hadn't considered the possibility of the two of them being thrown together, having to make polite talk, while trying not to think of all the intimacies they'd shared. After these past two days, nothing would ever be the same between them again.

"I don't know," he replied honestly.

His candid response gave her an opening she hadn't anticipated, an opportunity she wasn't going to let slip through her grasp. Scooting off the edge of the couch, she closed the physical distance between them. Emotionally, the gap seemed to widen. He watched her approach warily, but didn't bolt around her like she half expected him to when she stopped inches away.

Lifting her hand, she pressed her palm over his heart, absorbing the rapid pulse, and the warmth radiating off him. She inhaled his unique masculine scent, and her stomach curled with an acute desire and longing.

He stood statue still, giving her the impression that he wanted to prove that he was immune to her touch, to *her*. She'd give him an A for effort, but he ultimately failed to conceal his own need. She watched his pupils dilate into dark orbs, observed the slight flare of his nostrils that indicated just how aware of her he was...and just how hard he was struggling to keep that attraction and fascination confined.

Satisfied that she'd gotten to him, even just a tiny bit, she pushed her advantage, ignoring for the moment the promise she'd made—to be satisfied with nothing more than pleasure and erotic memories. "You might not know if you can handle seeing me at family gatherings, but I can tell you that after all we've shared, it won't be simple or easy for me. Not when I know what we had here in this cabin is worth taking a chance on."

Swearing viciously, he paced to the other end of the couch. "Dammit, I *knew* this would happen."

She tipped her head and regarded him cautiously. "You knew what would happen?"

His accusatory eyes burned like hot coals. "That you'd confuse lust with other sentimental emotions and want more from me than I can give you."

His anger and denials inflamed her own ire. All her life she'd been a mediator, rushing to diffuse angry flare-ups instead of dealing with whatever conflict or problem she encountered. It started with her parents, and gradually shaped her personality as she was growing up. She'd always been the one to soothe upsetting situations, restore peace and avoid opposition.

Being passive no longer held any appeal for her. Nor was she going to let Marc blame her for his own insecurities. He was battling his own fears and personal demons—she couldn't fight them, too, not unless she knew what they were.

Her chin lifted a determined notch. "If I learned one thing in this cabin with you, I now know the difference between satiating lust and making love. We did both, and I'm not confused about which took place when." She softened her tone, but not her candid words. "I'm not asking you for anything, but after our time together, and what we shared, I think I have the right to tell you how I feel."

"I do care for you, Brooke. And these past two days with you have been incredible, beyond anything I've ever experienced with any other woman." He scrubbed a hand over his jaw, looking torn. "As for taking a chance and pursuing this relationship any further than this cabin, I *can't.*"

She hadn't outright asked him to take that chance. She'd promised herself, and him, she wouldn't. But she couldn't suppress her curiosity. "Why not?" she countered. "And this time, give me a good, solid reason *why.*"

His brows snapped together, and his features swirled with dark, dangerous hostility. Unease slithered through Brooke. She'd never seen him this way before, never knew he possessed such depth and multi-faceted layers...and a secret he was very reluctant to share.

But then she'd never provoked him before. "Why not?" she asked again, forcing him to acknowledge her and the question.

His mouth flattened into a grim line. The emotions in his eyes were raw and frayed. "You want a good solid reason why? How about the fact that I'm just like my father, and Eric?"

The pit of her stomach clenched at his insinuation, but she refused to believe the worst, not after glimpsing shadows of old pain and regret in his eyes. "What, that you enjoy flattering women?"

"I wish it were as simple as that." Marc's shoulders slumped in defeat. He'd never meant for their special time together in this cabin to end on such a dreadful note, but she was leaving him little choice except to be brutally honest with her. "How about the fact that I have a problem remaining faithful?"

Her eyes widened and her hand fluttered to the collar of her sweater. "What?" she whispered, her soft voice colored with incredulity.

"It's true," he confirmed, and watched as a mixture of horror and disbelief creased her features. God, he hated hurting her. Hated that he was about to shatter the chivalrous image of him she'd believed in.

The fantasy was definitely over. They'd gone from friends, to lovers, and would quickly revert to polite acquaintances when she discovered he was too much like his brother.

Ignoring the growing pressure in his chest, he said, "Just like my father, and Eric, I've been unfaithful to someone I was seeing."

Slowly, she sank onto a sofa cushion. Her deep blue gaze, so filled with confusion, searched his expression, seemingly wanting to know more.

"That one indiscretion is enough to convince me that I'm not cut out for a monogamous, committed relationship, Brooke. Not long-term, anyway. Not when I take into consideration my father and brother's track record and what Eric put you through. I won't take that risk with *any* woman again. Especially you."

End of discussion for him, he stalked toward the front windows, searching for signs of the ranger's vehicle coming up the drive. No such luck. After two days of seclusion, he was feeling boxed in, edgy, and restless for wide open spaces. Though cabin fever would have been a logical excuse for his anxiety, he knew this unwanted conversation with Brooke was the real culprit.

"What happened?" she asked after long minutes passed.

Hanging his head, he shut his eyes, reaching deep for calm and patience. "You don't need to hear the sordid details." And he sure as hell didn't want to relive that awful night he'd spent the past eight years trying to forget.

"I want to know what happened," she persisted. "We've been nothing but honest with one another in this cabin. Before we leave, make me understand why these two days together are all we can have. I think you owe me that."

Yeah, he owed her an explanation for the brusque ending to their affair. And by the time he was done recounting his appalling tale, not only would she understand his reasons, she'd definitely keep her distance.

Bracing his arm on the frame above his head, he kept his gaze trained on a snow-covered tree outside, unable to look at Brooke, not wanting to see the pity in her eyes when he revealed the whole truth.

He inhaled a ragged breath, exhaled slowly. "Remember that survey question about one-night stands?"

"Yes," came her quiet reply from behind him.

"Well, that incident was it. One sexual encounter with a faceless stranger when I was still seeing another woman." He shook his head in disgust over his actions, and how that event had changed his entire view on serious relationships, as well as served to shore up the belief that short-term affairs were more his style.

He continued. "I was twenty-two at the time, and a senior in college. I'd been dating Dana Ramsey for about three months. She was ten years older than me, *very* experienced, and we spent most of our time together in bed. At first, I thought it was great. I mean, what healthy, hormonal twenty-two-year-old wouldn't?"

Brooke didn't answer him, but he wasn't expecting a reply to his rhetorical question. "Dana came on strong, was very possessive, clingy even, and I started feeling stifled. I told her I wasn't looking for anything serious, but that didn't seem to make a difference to her. If anything, my attempts to back out of the relationship intensified her demands."

He paused, remembering the panic he'd first experienced at Dana's pressure tactics, then the defiance that had settled in. "When she started dropping hints about us getting married, I just lost it and completely rebelled. I was at a frat party one night drowning my anxiety in beer. When some coed I didn't even know came on to me, I followed along and slept with her."

Silence settled over the room for several heartbeats, then Brooke spoke. "I take it that ended your relationship with Dana?"

He jerked his head around, unable to believe that she could be so apathetic about his infidelity. "Good God, Brooke, I felt like crap the next morning, knowing that I *cheated* on her. She didn't deserve that, no matter how uptight I was about her demands about marriage."

"True," she conceded, "but at least you experienced guilt and remorse after the fact."

He frowned. "What difference does that make?"

"You were young, you weren't ready to settle down, and you tried to tell Dana that, but she wouldn't listen," she said. "You made a mistake, Marc. One you obviously regret and haven't repeated."

How could she sit there and be so reasonable when he despised himself for what he'd done? "That doesn't excuse what I did."

"No, it doesn't," she agreed, but there was no condemnation in her expression.

"It's no better than what Eric did to you," he persisted.

"Don't compare yourself to your brother." Her gaze held his, filled with steely conviction. "You're two very different men, and the circumstances are completely different."

He gaped at her. "How can I *not* compare myself to Eric when I'm guilty of the same thing he did to you?"

"We were married, which makes a big difference. He *vowed* to be faithful to me." She stood, but didn't close the distance between them, opting instead to remain by the coffee table. "You were dating Dana, and she ignored your attempts to keep your relationship from getting too serious. And Eric cheated more than once, whereas this is your one and only indiscretion, an error of judgment that I'm guessing has been eating you up inside since it happened."

She knew him well. Too well.

Drawing a deep breath, she slid her fingers into the back pocket of her jeans. "And the biggest difference between you two? Eric and I never had the kind of openness and honesty and trust that you and I have shared in just two days."

And he'd never had that with any other woman, either, because he'd never let himself get close enough to establish those emotional bonds. Yet with Brooke, those intimacies had come naturally, and had felt incredibly right and good.

Turning back to the window, he pressed his fingertips to the cold pane. "I watched Eric get married to you, and I prayed that you'd be the one to keep him monogamous. And when it didn't happen, I lost all hope for myself." He swallowed the tight knot gathering in his throat. "I don't want to offer you false promises when I don't know if I can make that kind of commitment." But how he wished he *could* give her something more lasting and permanent.

"I'm not asking for a commitment, Marc," she said.

He laughed, but the harsh sound grated along his sensitive nerve endings. "Right at this moment, maybe not, but you will eventually. That's the kind of woman you are, and it's what you deserve." Pushing away from the window, he moved across the room toward her, prepared to issue more blunt and irrefutable honesty if that's what it took to make her understand, and leave this cabin with her own pride intact. "The sex between us was spectacular, but it won't be enough for you months down the road. You'll want more, and my biggest fear is that I'll panic again when things get too intense."

Her mouth quirked with the barest of smiles. "Things are already intense."

"And I'm *panicking!*" He felt himself physically trembling, and he pushed his unsteady hands through his disheveled hair. "I'm afraid of disappointing you, Brooke."

She bit her bottom lip, her eyes shining with a wealth of vulnerabilities. "And that's my same fear, that I'll disappoint you, too. That maybe I won't keep you satisfied in the long run. You don't own the market on insecurities."

He remained mute, stunned by her admission. Tenderness swelled within him, but before he could reassure her that she'd keep any man well gratified, she stepped toward him and pressed her palm to his bearded cheek, her touch, her eyes, unbearably gentle.

"But I'm most afraid of giving you up, of letting you go, of feeling empty and alone when you're gone." Her fingers grazed his jaw as if memorizing his features. "All my life I've done for everyone else. Now, I want to please *me*. There's more between us than incredible, mind-blowing sex. We both know it, feel it, even if you won't admit it out loud. I saw it in your eyes last night when we were making love. I see it in your eyes now."

Instinctively, he tried to turn his head away so she couldn't see straight to his soul, but she framed his face between both hands, not allowing him the luxury of that escape.

She stared deep into his eyes. "You want more than just an affair, I know you do. And I know you're afraid to take that risk, so I won't ask for more than you're willing to give. Making a relationship work isn't easy, but you have to want to try and make it happen. We could start out slow and simple, by seeing one another, and dating, and spending quality time together."

Overwhelming frustration gripped him. "To see if I'm capable of remaining committed in a relationship? To make sure I don't screw up again and hurt someone I—" He sucked in a swift breath, catching himself before the word *love* slipped past his lips and he gave her the leverage she needed to sustain her argument. His heart thudded in his chest, and he quickly amended his remark. "I don't want to risk hurting you."

"You make it sound like some kind of lab test," she quipped lightly.

"In a way, it would be a test. What if I discover that I can't handle being in a serious relationship? That I find I'm too restricted and I just can't commit? Where does that leave *you*?"

Instead of backing down, retreating or giving up on him like she should have done, she continued to fight. "I don't believe you'd deliberately hurt me. I don't believe you'd deliberately seek out another woman in an act of rebellion. Maybe when you were a young man of twenty-two who just wanted to have a good time in college and didn't want the responsibility of a relationship, but not now."

She paused, as if gathering her thoughts. Then she shared them. "I'll admit that I once believed you were

like Eric, too, but that was before I really took the time
to get to know you. I've discovered that you're a man
who has patience and likes to be around children.
You're warm, and caring, and you don't try to hide
who you are or try to be something you're not. The
Marc I know would cherish a wife and kids and work
through problems rather than shirk them."

Wife and kids. The very things he hadn't allowed himself to think about, but had always wanted. "You don't
know that."

"I *believe* it," she said with so much faith he almost
believed it, too. "The Marc I've learned about these
past two days isn't selfish. The Marc I've discovered
would put his family first, just as you're thinking of me
now, trying to protect me from something that may
never happen." She smiled, though the sentiment held
a tinge of sadness. "If your brother was half the man
you are, maybe Eric and I would still be married. And
maybe if I was the woman I am *now*, Eric never would
have felt the need to cheat."

"Eric was a damn fool," he said, meaning it.

A delicate brow lifted. "Then what does that make
you?"

An even bigger fool. "It would destroy me if I hurt
you, and I'm not willing to take that risk. For both our
sakes. If anything, I've learned from my father and
brother, and my own mistake." He headed over to the
front door, where they'd left their gear.

She trailed behind, more slowly. "Your father is still
married to your mother, and they're happy together.
They worked through whatever problems they had."

He slanted her a cynical look. "As you know from

your own parents' situation, it doesn't always end happily."

She stopped behind him, and crossed her arms over her chest. "What I do know, what I've learned, is that there's no guarantees in love and marriage. But if two people care enough to compromise and communicate, then love and a good, strong marriage *can* work."

The sound of a vehicle pulling into the drive echoed in the quiet cabin, followed by two short honks to announce the ranger's arrival.

Finally, Marc thought, welcoming the interruption, which saved him from issuing more arguments. "Sounds like our ride is here." He turned away, but she grabbed his arm and forced him to look at her.

"What if..." Her voice cracked, and she swallowed to ease her throat. "What if I tell you that I've fallen in love with you?"

He stared at her, seeing the devotion and hope shimmering in her eyes. Her sweet declaration nearly sent him to his knees with his own avowal, but he kept his emotions and his expression firmly battened down, even though he was dying inside. Anxiety banded his chest, but this time the pressure wasn't a result of feeling stifled, but because he dreaded the thought of spurning that love he ached for so badly.

He dredged up the words he knew he had to speak. "All the more reason to end this now." Scooping up her snowsuit and helmet from the floor, he handed them to her, then busied himself collecting his own gear.

Unable to look her in the eyes, he added, "I know this is difficult now, but in the long run, you'll thank me, Brooke."

THANK YOU VERY MUCH.

Brooke was thanking Marc, all right, for leaving her with a heartache she was certain would never ease. Two days, and she loved the man. Two days, and she was back to being alone again.

The emptiness and loss that consumed her was unlike anything she'd ever encountered. Her divorce from Eric had been inevitable. Losing Marc had been a one-sided choice she'd had little say in. He'd thwarted every argument, and ultimately rejected her, her love, and her belief in him—as if he knew what was best for her, all because he couldn't forgive himself for a past mistake.

Her gratitude was overwhelming.

When they'd returned to their cabin, he'd wasted no time in informing Shane and Ryan that they needed to hit the road so he could get back to his office since they were a day behind in returning. Within an hour, the men had vacated the place. Within five minutes of their departure Brooke knew her life would never be the same, not without Marc to complete it.

He'd taught her all about love and passion and embracing the woman inside her. And that woman wanted him, with the very depths of her heart and soul. She no longer wanted to live her life conservatively, and dreaded the boring, practical and predictable life-style awaiting her at home. Not when she'd tasted something far more exciting and thrilling with Marc.

She berated herself for her naiveté, for thinking she was capable of enjoying a fling with Marc and chalking the incident up as an unforgettable affair. She *did* crave more, more than he was willing to give.

"Come on, fess up, Brooke," Stacey cajoled. "We want all the steamy details."

Taking a deep breath and shaking off the desolate feeling swirling within her, Brooke sank down on the living room couch across from her friend and Jessica. "There's not much to tell," she hedged, not willing to divulge intimate details and sully what she'd shared with Marc. "Like I said, we got lost coming home from the lodge, ran out of gas, and had to break into someone's cabin for the duration of the storm."

"Sounds...*adventurous*."

Her friend's meaning was clear, but Brooke chose to ignore the underlying question in her comment. "We were lucky we found shelter, considering how brutal the blizzard turned out to be."

"And?" Stacey persisted.

Brooke affected nonchalance. "And what?"

Stacey blew out an exasperated stream of breath. "Well, did you two take advantage of the situation?"

In erotic, provocative ways she'd never imagined possible or would ever forget. Feeling Jessica's inquisitive gaze on her, as well, she laughed lightly to diffuse the anticipation seemingly quivering in the air. "Marc was a perfect gentleman." It wasn't a lie. He'd been generous with her pleasure, and entirely too noble about protecting her from himself.

Jessica didn't look completely convinced, and Brooke quickly averted her gaze from her sister's knowing one.

Stacey groaned in disappointment. "I can't believe you let a perfect opportunity like that go to waste!"

She shrugged as though to say "oh well" and

quickly changed the subject. "What about you and Shane?"

A dreamy expression softened Stacey's features. "Oh, we definitely took advantage of the situation."

Jessica rolled her eyes. "The two of them only came out of the downstairs bedroom to go to the bathroom or to the kitchen to get something to eat."

"Well, we certainly know who had the most fun on this trip." A grin lifted the corners of Stacey's mouth. "*And* I have a date with Shane when we return to Denver on Sunday."

Shaking her head in amusement, Brooke stood, ready to move past this conversation. "I think I'll make myself a sandwich. Anyone else?" The thought of food hitting her stomach made her queasy, but it worked as an excuse.

"None for me, thanks," Stacey said, reclining languorously on the couch. "I'm discovering that love has a way of eclipsing hunger."

"Love?" Brooke stared incredulously at her friend, who'd always avoided serious relationships in lieu of just having a good time. "You're in love with Shane?"

"Don't look so surprised. I know I come across as this wild, single woman, but when the right guy comes along there's no mistaking when it's the real thing."

Brooke felt a knot form in her chest, wishing that Marc could have had faith in the real thing. In her. "I'm happy for you."

Stacey's adoration for Shane shone in her eyes. "Thanks. I'm hoping it'll work out between us."

Heading into the kitchen, Brooke retrieved the lunch meat, cheese, bread and mayonnaise from the refrigerator and started making herself a sandwich. Admittedly, she wasn't really hungry, but starving herself over Marc wasn't something she'd allow herself to do.

"I'll take one," Jessica said from behind her as she entered the kitchen. "*My* hunger is still intact."

Brooke managed a smile at her sister's meaningful comment. She obviously hadn't fallen for Ryan Matthews's charm while she and Marc had been stranded. "How were things between you and Ryan during the blizzard?"

Jessica propped her hip against the counter next to Brooke. "Interesting, considering he didn't take much offense to my lawyer jokes." She sounded disappointed.

Slathering a piece of bread with spread, Brooke slanted her sister a sly look. "Hmm, smart guy." She gave Ryan credit, for seeing past Jessica's sassy mouth and attitude that kept men at arm's length.

Jessica reached for a slice of cheese and peeled off the plastic wrapper, her brows pulled into a troubled frown. "He asked me out," she said quietly.

Her confession took Brooke by surprise. "And?"

"I said no, of course," her sister replied quickly, layering slices of meat on their bread.

"Aw, Jess, you like him, don't you?" She'd always been able to read Jessica's moods and thoughts and felt pretty certain she'd accurately assessed her sister's problem.

"Maybe," she said nebulously. "I mean, he is a—"

"Lawyer," they finished at the same time.

"End of story," Jessica said succinctly. "I'm particular about who I date, and lawyers top the list of automatic no-gos."

Arguing Jessica's reasons was futile, Brooke knew.

"That's really too bad, because he seems like a nice guy."

She shrugged noncommittally as she finished stacking their sandwiches with ham.

Brooke brought down two small plates from the cupboard and Jessica set their lunch on them. "You know, you really shouldn't hold the guy's occupation against him."

"No matter how gorgeous, sexy or amusing I find Ryan, I don't like what he does for a living." A deep hurt shimmered in Jessica's eyes, brought on by old memories. "Why let myself get attached to him when it'll never work out?"

Just as Brooke had with Marc. She was attached...by the heart. "You'd be amazed at the things you'd be willing to compromise on if you fell for the right guy." Suddenly unable to eat even a bite of her sandwich, she pushed her plate away.

Jessica took a bite of her lunch, scrutinizing Brooke as she chewed. "Ohmigod," she said, her voice infused with a startling revelation. "Something *did* happen between you and Marc at that cabin. I knew it!"

She'd never lied to her sister, and she wouldn't do so now. "Yeah, something happened, but it's over before it's even had a chance to begin."

Jessica's brows rose in astonishment. "Did you two, um, *you know?*"

Brooke found the blush staining her sister's cheeks endearing. They'd talked about guys and sex, and from what Brooke knew, Jessica's experience was limited. "Yes, we made love, and it was the most incredible, intimate experience of my life." No doubt, no other man would ever compare to Marc.

"Wow," she murmured, envy tingeing her voice.

Brooke drew a deep breath, along with a healthy dose of fortitude. "And I love him."

"Oh, wow," Jessica said again, this time her eyes wide with concern. "What are you going to do?"

"There's nothing I can do. Marc knows how I feel about him, and he's decided that we're better off, that *he's* better off, not pursuing our relationship."

The compassion Brooke had offered Jessica so many times over the years was now returned by her sister. "I'm sorry, sis."

A bottomless sadness engulfed Brooke, tightening her vocal cords. "Yeah, me, too," she whispered.

12

MARC GLANCED at his watch, noted the time, and knew he couldn't avoid the inevitable much longer. He would have preferred spending Thanksgiving day holed up in his office, working on electrical estimates and generally being alone in his miserable state. Instead, he would soon be with Brooke at his parents', feigning that they were just friends and pretending that they hadn't spent two incredible days together that were indelibly etched in his mind. Regretting, too, the way he'd severed their affair and hurt her with his uncompromising conviction that ending their relationship was for the best.

Best for whom? his conscience taunted. The question had haunted him, tangling up his emotions with uncertainties and a yearning that tugged at his heart twenty-four hours a day.

Best for her, because he couldn't give her all that she deserved.

Best for him, to save himself from confronting fears he'd lived with for eight long years.

Tossing his pen onto his desk, he leaned back in his leather chair and stabbed his fingers through his disheveled hair. When had he become such a damn coward? Like a man who'd perfected the art of avoiding entanglements, he'd run hell-bent from the mere mention of commitment. Except no matter how hard he tried, he couldn't escape the fact that he'd fallen in love with Brooke.

The knowledge only compounded his misery. She was everything he'd ever wanted, and everything he knew he'd never have. While she might be willing to take risks with her future, and them, he was not. He knew he wasn't a smart investment for her, even if she wouldn't acknowledge that for herself.

Two weeks had passed since they'd been stranded together, and he hadn't heard from her. Not that he'd expected her to call when he'd given her no reason to hope that he might make room for her in his life. True to their agreement, she'd made no demands on him, and while he should have been grateful for her acquiescence, all he felt was a huge, gaping loss.

He straightened the contracts and files on his desk into neat piles. He reviewed bills, signed checks, and pitched wadded-up pieces of paper into the wastebasket. When he could stall no longer, he headed out of his office to his Suburban. On the way to his parents' place, on a whim he bought a bouquet of flowers from a roadside vendor to surprise his mother.

Once he arrived, he parked behind Eric's sports car. Brooke's vehicle wasn't in the drive, and he experienced relief that he'd been spared that initial awkward encounter, and disappointment at the thought that she might have decided to forgo the holiday with his family because of him.

Without knocking, he entered the two-story house he'd grown up in, hung his coat in the foyer closet, and followed the delicious aroma of Thanksgiving dinner toward the back of the house. He passed through the family room, and stopped at the glass slider leading to the back porch, where his father and Eric were practicing their putting skills on the strip of green his father used in the wintertime to perfect his short-range shots. Marc knocked and waved a greeting.

He started on his way, then paused when he caught sight of the family portrait that still hung on the paneled wall. The picture had been taken when he was sixteen, and Eric eighteen, about six months before his parents' marriage had hit its lowest point, if he remembered correctly.

He stepped closer to the portrait, noticing how he and Eric were positioned between their mother and father. His parents were both smiling at the camera, but their eyes held no joy, and their expressions were more strained than relaxed. He shook his head, amazed that he'd never noticed those small telltale signs before now, and realized what they'd signified. Amazed, too, that the man and woman in the portrait didn't resemble the loving couple his parents were now, despite the rough times they'd endured. All these years he'd taken his parents' marriage for granted, never giving much thought to how much work they'd put into the relationship to make it last, when they easily could have opted for a divorce during that crisis.

Mulling that over, he continued through the house and found his mother in the kitchen. She was standing by the stove wearing an apron over her casual khaki pantsuit, stirring a simmering pot of what looked and smelled like gravy. He approached quietly from behind and presented the flowers first.

"Happy Thanksgiving, Mom."

Kathleen whirled around, surprise lighting her features when she saw him. "Happy Thanksgiving to you, too." She gave him a hug and a kiss on the cheek, then reached for the bouquet and inhaled the floral fragrance. "Oh, honey, they're beautiful, but you shouldn't have!"

Her words meant she was thrilled that he'd thought of her, he knew. "I wanted to." He shrugged and grinned, and for the first time in two weeks felt a lightness in his heart. "I like seeing you smile."

She beamed, her blue eyes sparkling with pleasure. "You're just like your father," she said, and turned away to retrieve a vase from the cupboard.

After the heavy discussion he and Brooke had had at the cabin, his mother's comment initially startled him, and made him wonder, exactly, what she meant by her comparison. He wanted to ask, but wasn't sure how to phrase the question without sounding defensive.

Heading to the refrigerator, he retrieved a bottle of beer, screwed off the top, and took a drink of the malty liquid. "Is Brooke coming today?" he asked as nonchalantly as possible.

"Yes." She filled the cut crystal vase with water, and unwrapped the flowers, arranging the stems just so. "And I invited Jessica, too, so she wouldn't have to spend the day alone. Brooke called just before you got here and said she was running a little behind. She should be here in about half an hour."

His stomach did a tiny flip. Automatically, he glanced at the clock on the wall and gauged the time, and just how long it would be before he saw her again.

Kathleen glanced his way. "Do you plan on going outside to visit with Eric and your father?"

He shook his head, still trying to figure out a casual

way to ask his mother why she thought he was so much like his dad. "I saw them on my way to the kitchen and waved hello."

Picking up the vase, she passed him to the adjoining dining room, where she set the arrangement in the center of the formal mahogany table they used on special occasions, then returned. "Well, if you plan on staying in here, I'm going to put you to work."

He set his beer aside, and pushed up the sleeves of his cable-knit sweater. "That's fine, just so long as you don't make me wear an apron."

"Why not?" Her eyes sparkled playfully. "Your father looks very cute wearing my aprons." She laughed. "Of course your father would never admit that he's ever worn one, but, well, baking with your father can get really messy, but fun."

To his dismay, he felt his face warm. "I'm *sure* I don't want to hear this."

She retrieved two pot holders from a drawer and handed them to him, then opened the oven for him to retrieve the turkey. "What, you think just because we're an old married couple that we don't have any fun together?"

That sobered him, because there had been a time when his parents hadn't enjoyed one another's company. Hefting the huge, golden-brown turkey from the oven, he set it on the stove top. "I'm really glad that you and Dad have each other." He meant that sincerely, and couldn't imagine his parents apart...*now*.

She shut the oven door, her expression softening. "Me, too, though I'm sure you know our marriage wasn't always so pleasant."

He'd never discussed with either his mother or fa-

ther the obvious problems they'd endured years ago,
though at the time he and Eric had been old enough to
decipher their arguments, and figure out the gist of
what was going on. They just hadn't known the details,
the reasons why their parents had drifted apart, or
what had brought them back together.

"What happened?" he asked, surprising both of
them with his frank question.

She didn't shy away from his personal query, but
then he knew she wouldn't. Over the years his mother
had developed a strength and candidness he now appreciated.

"Well," she said, taking a deep breath, and keeping
her gaze steadily on him. "Do you remember the hysterectomy I had when you and Eric were in high
school?"

Marc nodded. "Yes."

"Well, that's where the problems started in our marriage." She gave a small smile, and uncovering the
fresh yams she'd baked, she layered the top with pecans. "After the surgery, I experienced some depression, mostly because I didn't feel desirable anymore.
I'll admit that your father was very understanding at
first, but I kept pushing him away and wouldn't talk to
him about how I was feeling. Eventually, we grew
apart, emotionally and physically, and instead of
working on the problem together, I completely shut
out your father because of my own insecurities. Before
long, we were like two strangers living in the same
house."

Marc was surprised to learn of the deeper issues that
had contributed to his parents' troubled marriage. As a
teenager, he'd noticed his mother's mood swings, but

had never known the extent of her illness, or how it had affected his father. All he'd seen and learned of had been the affair that had ultimately brought his mother and father to a crossroad in their relationship.

Kathleen's delicate brow wrinkled as she pulled out more memories to share. "And then one night your father came home and told me he'd had an affair. He was so wracked with guilt and remorse, and of course I was completely devastated."

"How did you get through that?" Marc asked.

"It wasn't easy, that's for sure." She gave a little laugh, but Marc knew that incident must have been a very painful time for both of them. "I wanted to blame your father for the affair, but the truth was, I was more at fault for pushing him away and forcing him to look elsewhere for what his own wife wouldn't give him. It's not an excuse for what he did, but it was his honesty about the situation that made me realize just how close I was to losing him. He could have kept that one night a secret or continued with the affair or had numerous ones, but he didn't. It wasn't what he wanted."

She sprinkled brown sugar on top of the yams and pecans, and continued. "The experience made us re-evaluate our marriage and forced us to decide what we were going to do. When I suggested a divorce, thinking that's what your father wanted, he broke down and told me that he wanted me, and us, the way we were when we first got married."

Marc reached for the bag of marshmallows on the counter and placed them on the top of the candied yams. He recognized the true meaning of commitment in the way his parents had worked through their troubles, instead of opting for the easy way out. "And you wanted that, too."

"Yes, I did." She smiled without an ounce of regret for the choice she'd made. "But first, I had to get help for my depression, which I did. And as we talked and worked through the mess we'd made of our marriage, we discovered that we had never stopped loving one another. With everything that happened after my hysterectomy, I just lost track of what was most important, and that was your father, our marriage, you and Eric, and being a family."

Once again, she opened the oven, and he placed the baking dish on the rack so the marshmallows could melt over the yams. They'd been open about everything else, now he wanted an answer to the question he hadn't been able to voice earlier.

He tipped his head toward his mom. "What did you mean about me being just like Dad?"

She rummaged through a cupboard and brought down the box that held the electric knife for carving the turkey, and cast a smile his way. "I only meant that you're thoughtful, sweet and sensitive."

"Sweet? Sensitive?" He blanched. "Uh, that's not usually how guys like to be described."

She laughed as she unrolled the cord to the knife. "What, you want me to tell you how macho and strong and handsome you are?"

He grinned. "I'll take strong and handsome."

"All the men in this family are that, but you, well, you take after your dad in so many ways." Warmth and affection touched her features. "I love Eric, but he just doesn't have that sensitivity to other people's feelings that you and your father do, which I think is part of the reason his marriage to Brooke didn't work. I also believe that he gave up so easily and settled for divorce because it just wasn't true love between them. Otherwise, he would have fought for her."

Undying, true love. Marc loved Brooke and he hadn't fought for her. His chest tightened with too many emotions, too many fears...the biggest one of which was living the rest of his life without Brooke.

"Being thoughtful, and considerate, and caring is a compliment, Marc," his mother continued, oblivious to his internal turmoil. "It makes you the kind of man a woman can trust and rely on because you'd never intentionally hurt her, just like your father never set out purposely to hurt me all those years ago. And someday, when the right woman comes along, those qualities will make you a wonderful husband and she'll be very lucky to have you."

Marc leaned against the counter as his mother turned away to check on the gravy. He absorbed her words, feeling as though he'd been sucker-punched in the stomach.

God, what had he done? Hadn't Brooke tried to tell him essentially the same thing his mother was telling him now? And just like his mother, Brooke believed in him, too—saw the goodness and honesty and integrity he swore had been stripped away that night he'd made the wrong decision.

He'd been so wrapped up in the past, so fearful that he'd repeat that same mistake with Brooke, that he couldn't bring himself to trust his true instincts, or grasp that unending faith she had in him. Instead, he'd used that youthful mistake and his father's indiscretion as a barrier, intent on punishing himself for the guilt and regret that had consumed him. And in the process he'd lost the one and only woman he'd ever loved.

For eight years, he'd considered being like his father a curse, not knowing his dad's affair had been prompted by emotional issues with his mother. Now, he saw the qualities he'd inherited from his dad for the blessings they were, and was grateful for the strength it gave him to trust himself, to know that he *could* endure the hard times...with the right woman to complement him.

The doorbell rang, and his mother's face lit up. "That must be Brooke and Jessica. Why don't you go answer the door while I check the yams and call your brother and father inside?"

Marc couldn't move. That damnable fear again. But this time he dreaded the worst, that his blunder in doubting Brooke, in not trusting her, in rejecting her love, would result in the biggest mistake of his life.

What if he'd hurt her so badly she no longer wanted him? Could he blame her? Could he live without her? Did he even stand a chance at reclaiming her love?

The doorbell rang again. "Marc?" his mother said, frowning at him. "Would you please get the door?"

"Uh, yeah," he said, and forced himself to move toward the foyer. Heart hammering wildly, he opened the door, and time stood still as he devoured the sight of Brooke.

Their gazes met, hers a soft, velvet shade of blue. He searched for a sign that she still wanted him, that she forgave him for not believing in her. Before he could witness anything to give him a glimmer of hope, she glanced away, as if it pained her to look at him.

His heart dropped to his stomach.

Jessica cleared her throat, breaking the silence and the tension that thrummed in the air between him and Brooke. "Happy Thanksgiving, Marc. Do you plan on inviting us in?"

"I, uh, yeah, come on in." He opened the door wider so they could enter.

Jessica stepped through the threshold first and gave him a sisterly hug in greeting. He turned toward Brooke, who watched him warily. Then, with amazing fortitude and frustrating detachment she gave him a hug, too—but she was holding a pumpkin pie in the crook of her arm and used it to her advantage, to keep a discreet distance between them. He couldn't wrap his arms around her waist and pull her close like he ached to, not without crushing the dessert she'd brought. The only part of their bodies that touched was the hand she settled lightly around his back, and the press of their shoulders. Quick, impersonal, but her scent, mingled with the fragrant scent of cinnamon and spice, lingered long after she moved away.

"Can I help with your coat?" he offered, dying for an excuse to *really* touch Brooke, to feather his fingers along her neck, to run his hands down her arms, and see if there was a spark of anything left between them. Lord knew just the sight of her made his pulse race and desire heat his blood.

She quickly shook her head and moved out of his reach, as if remembering the kiss that had transpired the last time he'd helped her with her coat in this very foyer. "No, thank you."

Handing the pie to Jessica, who slanted him a look

that said *sorry, buddy, but you blew it,* Brooke shrugged out of her coat and hung it in the closet next to Jessica's.

"It looks and feels like it might snow tonight," Brooke said, her voice holding no real emotion that he could grasp. Nothing to bolster his optimism that he might still stand a chance with her.

The weather? She was talking about the *weather?* So formal. So polite. So distant and reserved. Aggravation flowed through him, along with an acute sense of loss. The flirtatious banter and easy conversation he'd once enjoyed with her was a thing of the past. As were they, it seemed.

What did he honestly expect after the abrupt way he'd ended things with her? She was holding up her end of their agreement, making no demands, acting as though they hadn't spent two days stranded together, pretending that she hadn't learned more about him than any woman had ever taken the time or care to discover.

And he hated her aloofness. He wanted the warm, sweet, generous Brooke back. The one who gave of herself so freely. The one who'd pried open his heart and given him the faith and love he'd so desperately needed.

But he'd shunned her selfless offering, her priceless trust, and he had no idea how to repair the damage he'd done.

COMING HERE hadn't been a good idea. Brooke forced another swallow of stuffing and gravy, wishing that she'd followed her original plan to call Kathleen with the excuse that she wasn't feeling well, and skip Thanksgiving dinner with the Jamisons. Except Jessica wouldn't let her take the easy way out, and promised her it would get easier in time to be around Marc if she didn't avoid situations with him now.

But it hurt like hell to be near Marc, to even look at him, because all she could think about was how much she loved him, with everything she had within her, and that she had to live the rest of her life with the knowledge that he'd never be hers.

She'd spent the past hour since arriving avoiding eye contact with Marc and casually skirting him when he came near. It had been awkward enough at the door; she could only imagine how strained and uncomfortable it would be if they were caught in the position of being alone. Any conversation with him had been in a group with other members of his family, and very superficial on her part.

She'd smiled and endured, as she was now at the dinner table while everyone else carried on a lively conversation. She had no clue why Marc was brooding across from her when she'd abided by their agreement to resume their friendship. No pressure, no demands, no promises.

She was going to leave just as soon as it was politely possible, she decided as she took a bite of her buttered roll. And she would arm herself with a multitude of excuses to avoid Christmas with the Jamison family.

A lull came over the current conversation, and Eric transferred his gaze from Marc to Brooke. "You know, you two seem awfully quiet this evening," he commented. "And I don't think I've seen you say two words to one another. Did you guys have a fight while you were stranded together?"

"No," she and Marc answered in quick unison, hers a soft reply and his a rough bark.

Eric quirked a brow at Marc, scrutinizing his brother with his direct look. "What has *you* so uptight?"

Marc stabbed his fork into a slice of turkey and scowled at his brother. "I am *not* uptight."

"Yes, you are," Kathleen cut in, agreeing with Eric. "You were fine earlier when we were talking in the kitchen...until, well, Brooke arrived."

Four pairs of eyes glanced her way, and she felt her skin prickle and heat. She managed an impish shrug. She couldn't imagine what she'd done to make him so upset, unless he resented that she'd come at all. What else could it be?

"We're fine, really." Her reassurance only seemed to annoy Marc more.

His father redirected the conversation, recounting an amusing tale of a Thanksgiving when Eric and Marc had been kids and the two of them hid a few of their plastic army men in the hollowed-out turkey when Kathleen hadn't been looking, and what a surprise it had been to find them in the stuffing. Everyone laughed but Marc.

Eric continued to watch Marc, and Brooke knew that stare—it was the kind of look that said he'd found an intriguing mystery he wanted to decipher.

Finally, Marc bristled. *"What?"* he snapped at his brother, surprising everyone with his abrupt outburst.

"Man, I've never seen you like this before." Eric shook his head in bafflement. "It's got to be a woman that has you so on edge and moody."

Marc dropped his fork onto his plate. "So what if it is?"

Brooke's stomach churned at the challenging note in Marc's voice, but Eric merely chuckled at his brother's dark tone and slapped him on the back. "It's hell when women aren't cooperative, isn't it?"

"It's not her, it's *me*," Marc admitted, sounding just as miserable as Brooke felt, though he never looked her way. Indeed, it was as though she wasn't even in the room. "I'm the one who blew it, and I'm afraid that nothing I say or do will change her mind about me, or us."

The thudding of Brooke's heart roared in her ears as she tried to make sense of his comment and this little drama playing out before her—which made no sense at all. Reaching numbly for her glass of wine, she took a big gulp to drown the swarm of unease churning in her belly.

Kathleen gazed at her youngest son, her eyes filled with gentle wisdom. "Have you told her how you feel about her?"

"No," Marc replied, his voice hoarse with regret. "I was too much of a coward the last time we were together."

"A woman needs to know how her man feels about her." Kathleen shared a loving look with her husband, who sat at the other end of the table from her. "The next time you see her tell her exactly how you feel."

Marc stood, and Brooke fully expected him to leave the dinner table with his dignity and pride still intact—and her heart in shreds. It was all she could do not to bolt herself.

He looked straight at her, his gray eyes brimming with an odd combination of nerves and gentleness. "I

love you, Brooke," he said in a voice so clear and pure
she knew she had to be dreaming.

The commotion that erupted at the table assured her
she was not.

"Oh, my goodness," his mother exclaimed softly.

"I'll be damned," his father said in surprised amusement.

"*Finally*," Jessica muttered.

"No kidding?" Eric asked, his expression amazed.

"No kidding," Marc affirmed softly, hopefully. "I
love you, Brooke." He waited anxiously for her response.

An overwhelming rush of emotion swelled within
her, joy, anticipation and stunned disbelief that he'd
blurted out his feelings in front of his family. Not willing to discuss something so personal with everyone
watching and listening, she stood and calmly set her
napkin on the table. "I think this is something that
would be better discussed in private."

Marc watched Brooke leave the dining area and
head toward the family room, his chest tightening with
an awful, heart-stopping pressure. Her composed, formal attitude wasn't the reaction he'd been expecting or
hoping for, and he couldn't help but fear that he was
too late with his declaration.

Eric broke the strained silence that had descended
over the dinner table with Brooke's departure. "I have
to admit, Brooke was the last woman I expected you to
be tied up in knots over."

Marc glanced at his brother, realizing how ironic it
was that he'd once envied his brother for having
Brooke, and now had fallen deeply, irrevocably in love
with that same woman. "She's an incredible woman,"

he said, though he knew that one adjective didn't do Brooke justice.

"Yeah, she is pretty incredible," Eric agreed quietly, but sincerely. "So make sure you treat her better than I did." Smiling, he held out his hand toward Marc in a gesture of respect and consent to the relationship.

Marc shook his brother's hand, and one quick look around the table affirmed that everyone else approved, as well.

"Just as a father-to-son piece of advice," his dad offered, casting an affectionate glance toward his wife. "It's been my experience that women like it when men wear their heart and emotions on their sleeve. You've made a good start of that here in this room, but it doesn't stop once you've got her. Make sure she knows that you love and cherish her...every day."

Kathleen smiled. "I can attest to that excellent advice."

The support and encouragement of his family went a long way in restoring his fortitude with Brooke. Heading into the family room, he saw Brooke standing there looking so achingly beautiful, so vulnerable and uncertain, and did the only thing he knew would assure her that he meant the love he'd professed to her in the other room.

Closing the distance between them, he caught her up in his arms and wrapped her in his strength and warmth. And then he kissed her, from the very depths of his heart, body and soul. The embrace was like coming home after being gone for an eternity.

When he broke the kiss, he framed her soft, smooth cheeks in his hands and tipped her face up to his, so he could look into her eyes. "I meant what I said, Brooke. I *do* love you."

"I know," she whispered, a tremulous smile touching her mouth. "I knew you loved me at the cabin, and I was so afraid that you'd never admit it, or see it for yourself."

"What can I say. I was an idiot. I didn't want to hurt you, but I put us both through hell by pushing you out of my life." And now, he was ready to tackle the next hurdle with her. "Brooke...I want to take that chance with you."

A small frown formed on her brow. "Why?"

She had every right to ask, to know what had changed his mind. He settled his hands on her hips to keep her close. "For the past eight years I've carried around guilt and blame, and a whole lot of fear. It was easier for me to keep my distance and not get emotionally involved with anyone than risk screwing up again. And then you came along and blasted through every defense I had, believing in me, trusting in me, when I couldn't even trust myself."

He pressed his forehead to hers, inhaled a deep breath, then went on. "I have to be honest with you, Brooke. I'm not this miraculously changed person. I still harbor insecurities and I still have doubts, but I see that fear as a good thing. It makes me a stronger person, and more aware of how hard I have to work to make *us* work. I don't ever want to take you for granted, or lose sight of what's important to me, and that's *you*."

"Don't you think all this scares me, too?" she asked, seemingly humbled by all he'd revealed. "But I do trust you, and I believe in you. But most of all, I love you, too."

"God, I don't think I'll ever get tired of hearing that." He kissed her, slow and deep and rich with promise.

Moments later, she insisted against his warm lips, "I want dates, lots of them."

He grinned as his mouth skimmed across her cheek, thinking of all the places he wanted to take her, of all the fun they'd have together. "I think I can arrange that."

She tilted her head back, giving him better access to nuzzle her neck. "I want to take things slow and easy."

"Hmm. Slow and easy can be good." He felt the shiver that coursed through her at the sexy, husky insinuation in his voice, and he wished they were back at the cabin, naked and alone.

"Nothing serious or restricting—"

"No."

His firm tone startled her, and she looked up into his face. "What do you mean, no? I just thought..."

"That's what I wanted?" he cut in quickly. "That we'd see where all this might lead?"

She swallowed, confusion coloring her eyes. "Well, yes."

He shook his head adamantly. "Do you honestly think I'm going to date you, make love to you often, every day if possible, and not insist on a commitment from you?" He didn't wait for her to answer. "It's all or nothing, Brooke. When I make my mind up about something, I'm not a man who does it halfway."

"Another reason to love you." A slow, joyful grin

blossomed. "All right, then how about we have a hot, sexy, *exclusive* fling?"

The grin he gave her was as wicked as the hands easing beneath her blouse, stroking her skin, making her melt and moan just for him. "Yeah, I like the sound of that, just so long as the fling lasts for the next fifty years or so."

She laughed, knowing they were destined for a future filled with happiness, love, and incredible, unbelievable passion.

*Be sure to look for Jessica and Ryan's
sexy, fun-filled story in
SEDUCED, Temptation "Blaze" #811
by Janelle Denison.
Available December 2000.*